# THE END. AND AGAIN

DINO BAUK

# THE END.
# AND AGAIN

Translated from the Slovene by
Timothy Pogačar

First published in 2019 by **Istros Books**
(in collaboration with Beletrina Academic Press)
London, United Kingdom
www.istrosbooks.com

Originally published in Slovene as *Konec. Znova* by Beletrina Academic Press, 2015

Translation © Timothy Pogačar

Cover design and typesetting: Davor Pukljak | www.frontispis.hr

ISBN: 978-1-912545-28-5

This Book is part of the EU co-funded project *"Reading the Heart of Europe"*
in partnership with Beletrina Academic Press | www.beletrina.si

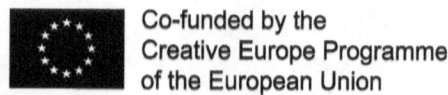

Co-funded by the
Creative Europe Programme
of the European Union

The European Commission support for the production of this publication does not constitute an endorsement
of the contents which reflects the views only of the authors, and the Commission cannot be held responsible
for any use which may be made of the information contained therein.

# CONTENTS

*For Maja, who, since I was of Denis's age,*
*smiles at me from the passenger seat and*
*for Urban, Gašper and Uroš,*
*who are, one over the other,*
*constantly taking to us in the rear-view mirror.*

"There were six of them: four men and two blond girls.
They stood, seemingly scattered across the hill, but Kate
recognized the pattern. She walked passed one of the men and
saw nothing in his eyes. Another step and she found herself
in her place. At that moment she heard the silence.
And she started singing the silent song."
DAVID ALBAHARI, *Silent Song*

# DENIS, 1989

He liked foggy autumn evenings when he could see only what was very close by. In that small world of a metre radius, bordered by walls of condensed moisture with no room for anyone else, he could pretend he was alone: on the street, in the city, in the world. He could see only a step or two ahead, and his small world moved with him, as if a round cluster of yellow lights were following him across a dark stage. At first, he heard only the quiet, dull steps of other people approaching him. They become gradually louder, and then for just an instant, black shadows cut through the foggy wall and fell aside. He could even pass by people he knew in the fog without having to say hello or strike up boring, polite conversations. To be honest, most people got on his nerves. He was sixteen: old enough for cigarettes, alcohol, and evenings out, but not enough for genuine independence. He had long grown tired of being accountable to his old man and mum. The one-and-a-half room flat on the thirteenth floor of a twenty-floor high-rise on the North Side seemed smaller to him by the day. It was only bearable when no one moved about much, when his old man drowsed in front of the TV, his mum busied herself tidying up the kitchen and lit a cigarette at the big dining table, and he was in his room listening to music with earphones, reading, or inaudibly, so to say, fingering chords on his guitar without really strumming the silent strings with his right hand. Most of the time he felt the flat was unbearably crowded, even though there were only three people living there. It was as if each day the ceiling dropped another millimetre to the floor, and the walls came a millimetre closer. He lacked air. He had an urge to go out, onto the street, into the cold evening, into his foggy refuge. Evening after evening, he and his old man played out a set ritual to the last detail like two veteran actors. They staged the one-act street theatre for themselves and for his mum, when she didn't work second shift. When he was almost to the door, after having pulled on a worn field jacket, black cap in one hand and the other on the latch, his old man called from the living room in his native Serbo-Croatian.

'Denis! Where you off to again?'

'To town.'

'Why the hell are you wandering around town like some bum? You want to be in trouble with the police again?'

For his old man there was no real difference between the police giving him a warning during a routine patrol and them seizing him in front of a burgled duty-free shop with a bag full of imported cigarettes, whiskey, and chocolates. Having anything to do with them meant being guilty of something – if nothing else, of wandering about aimlessly and uselessly in the evening, which of course cast his parents in a bad light even more than him, being that his old man lived in a world that respected all manner of authority. This had been his old man's new, constant worry ever since two policemen had stopped him on a walk around the North Side, asked who was writing the graffiti on the walls, and carefully took down his details. Someone (and of course Denis knew full well who) had written 'Fuck off Poland' on a white wall. The graffiti, hastily written in black spray paint, seemed to the policemen, not to mention to the concerned citizen who reported it to them, and probably to most adults on the North Side, as like something aimed against the government, or at least against a friendly socialist country, a complaint.

In fact, it was a wholly innocent and senseless piece of slang that had caught on among North Side teenagers at the time. One evening, someone had probably tossed it off at some gathering, a second and third person used it on some other occasion, repeating it in some gathering, and it entered into general use. Kids on the North Side now said 'Fuck off Poland' instead of the boringly simple, 'Addio'. Of course, Denis didn't start explaining this to the two men of the law. In a certain sense, he was amused at how terribly dangerous the quickly scrawled lettering seemed to the two of them. Its author probably forgot about it the day after conspiratorially applying it to the wall in the dark. On the other hand, it was really pretty careless to tell his parents about his talk with the men in blue, thinking he would share with them his rage at the gratuitous harassment, and he damn well regretted it the instant his old man exploded in agitation, shooting from the living room couch into the kitchen.

Since then, his old man, who was mostly worried about possible troubles at the army base on his account, reminded him almost every time he went out in the evening to be careful not to get a warning. He was convinced that every such entry in a vigilant policeman's notebook would be preserved forever somewhere deep in the state's administrative bowels, and that if it turned out to be needed, it could be spat out into the daylight at any time. Yeah, the world his old man lived in was a world of constant surveillance that wasn't carried out by some big brother's all-seeing eye with the aid of the state security service's cameras and microphones: the whole thing was much less sophisticated, actually quite simple, and thus the more effective.

'Don't worry about it. I'm going to a concert, be back by twelve.'

He pulled the door and it closed much more loudly that he expected. The light in the hallway always went out when he was waiting for the lift to reach the twelfth floor. He never turned it on again so through the crack he could see his shadow on the steel doors in the shaft's darkness just before it was filled with the lift car's neon light. From beneath the basement stairs leading to the shelter to which not one of the building's residents believed they would actually flee in fear in the near future, he took his cigarettes and lighter from hiding, and as was his habit, opened the building door with an elbow, having already lit up, and exited with a kind of half circle step. The cold evening air, to which smog and cheap coal lent a characteristic Ljubljana charm, filled his nostrils and mouth, and then his lungs, along with the first draw on the Winston. He thought of it as the smell of freedom: a mixture of gloom, cold, fog, and cigarette smoke. He was alone on the street, blanketed with a thick cloak of fog that hid him from familiar and unfamiliar passers-by. The walk to the bus stop lasted one cigarette. A scrawny young man with glasses, a little older than him, and a girl, were already there. Must be some student, Denis thought – only fucking students wear black sweaters and coats with badges that announce they care about things, that they're 'active'. They care about free speech, they care about dolphins, they care about Tibetan monks, they care about the Amazon rainforests, they care about the Kosovo miners, they care about Chinese students, and they care about Janša, the local journalist who supposedly swiped some secret documents from the army and published them. He remembered the skinny guy from school a few years ago as one of the punks in leather jackets fitted out with chains, cigarettes always in their mouths. They seemed pretty scary to Denis, who was several years younger, like some kind of ghouls from below ground. He was scared of them, even though they never paid him any attention. Now, having returned from the army, the lanky guy looked more like a wildly unkempt hippy than a punk. The good old Yugoslav National Army had clearly somewhat castrated him too, something

Denis and his classmates in the neighbourhood often noticed with those who returned from the service. When Denis came up next to them, the guy was in the middle of explaining to the student how disappointed he was with the turnout to the benefit concert for Janša and his three co-defendants. All the while he nervously puffed on a cigarette, as if labouring to finish it before the bus came. There was no sign that the student was interested in what he was saying. Maybe the topic would have drawn her in, but the accidental acquaintance was obviously more than getting on her nerves, so she just nodded, very attentively looking down the street for the bus to finally arrive. They hadn't come together; the hippy had obviously ambushed her unawares when she was waiting at the stop. Denis was amused by the fact that the student wouldn't evade the burden of the guy in glasses even when the bus came, since the character would surely stick to her and torture her for at least another eight stops with his theorizing.

The bus that would take him, the hippie, and the student downtown drove up empty. The hippy and the bored student sat somewhere in the middle and he kept up his boring monologues, while she, resigned to her fate, waited for her stop to rescue her.

Denis always sat in the back of the bus, in the last row. That way he had a view of what was happening. He like watching total strangers getting on and off, guessing their occupations, and imagining their stories. He was sorry for some, because they obviously were destined for a statistician's role in life, and others he envied, because it seemed to him they were more fortunate than he when roles were assigned, although he thought he was playing one of the leads. He believed he wouldn't pass through life unnoticed, though he hadn't the faintest idea how he would rise above the ordinary. Perhaps the underground band with Peter and Goran, that was taking more and more of his free time would make it, although they were long hours of practice from their first performance. He never dreamed that several years later, upset by the crowd, he would leave the line at the window for getting citizenship and become completely invisible. And that several years after that he and those like him would be called the 'erased'.

His mind went back to earlier that day, when he was sitting in the same back seat of the bus, and watching people come on. A blinding sun, that for a short interval after the morning fog dispersed, and before the afternoon fog would fall in an hour or two, reigned over Ljubljana and pierced the large, spattered windows. The bus filled only through the front door, by the driver, who had just taken off his green winter uniform jacket and was slowly rolling up the sleeves of his striped shirt as he carefully checked passengers' monthly passes through his sunglasses. Since it was not yet the hour of mass exodus from downtown towards the suburbs, only a few school pupils and retirees got on. And then Denis spotted her: at the end of the line getting on, in a group of four uniformed young people. She got on last, after two young men and a girl in white shirts and dark coats. He recognized them by the black tags on their chests.

'Hey, morons.'

He had noted their arrival in the city not long before. Young Americans his age and a little older started ambushing him sometimes on the way from school, on the pavements downtown, which they clearly chose as ideal traps. Until now he had only met male representatives. They seemed like a joke to him because of their polish, the complete opposite of his image of young people from the cradle of rock 'n roll. They lay in wait – flawlessly parted hair, pressed pants, and fixed smiles – for passers-by and tried to explain Jesus Christ's final days or something like that in fairly good Slovene, if tinged with an American accent.

Dropping a few coins in the box by the driver, she first gave him a smile, and then turning and heading through the bus, she did the same to all the other passengers, including Denis. He could have watched her, like many people before, and tried to guess her story, maybe catch her eyes for a moment, even smile at her, and then, after getting off, march away from the whole thing with yet another pleasant sketch in the collection of moments that wouldn't immediately be wiped away, but float there for some time, and every once in a while elicit a melancholy sigh. But she was a Mormon: contact with her should like as not be avoided, not sought. A quick look in her direction, which one of the young men also caught, was enough for the entire Mormon platoon to approach him. Although she was still in the back, he tried to catch her eyes, as if not noticing the other three, and not responding to their well-rehearsed introductions, 'I'm brother so-and-so, he's brother so-and-so.' Only she interested him.

'So you must be sister something?'

'I'm Mary.'

'Of course, the Virgin Mary, who else?'

He felt that his childlike laugh didn't anger, but amused her. She rewarded him with a changed, teasing smile, which fuelled his courage. He rose from his seat to take an equal place among the small group and push closer to her as she stood behind her two brothers and sister. One of the two slick assholes tried to guide the conversation, but Denis was communicating with her only, turning the other three Mormons into useless appendages, which they themselves understood after several stops, and gradually retreated into their own conversation.

He was finally one on one with the playful smile that betrayed curiosity and at the same time, like a raging river, easily overflowed its defensive levees. The bus engine, fortified with the hissing and groaning of the well-worn brakes, wrapped their conversation in an airtight sound curtain that rose for a few seconds at every stop, making it audible to the other passengers, especially the remainder of the Mormon expedition.

'I'll let you tell me all about your God, but first you have to let me take you to my church', he said at one of the stops, once the bus completely halted, and he caught the questioning look that one of the brothers sent to Mary. The bus set off once again, and the continuation of their conversation was drowned in the roar. The brother's attentive eyes were on Mary all the way to the stop where the platoon got off.

Back in the present, the student pronounced 'I'm getting off here', at the same stop at which Denis had agreed to meet with Mary at the end of their unexpected mutual commute. Denis wasn't fully convinced that she would actually show up. When in the morning he had invited her to meet, she responded with open interest and quiet assent, followed immediately by a quick guilty look at the brother who was watching her with most concern during their conversation. Because of that brief reality check, when for a moment she broke eye contact, Denis later wondered whether she was serious or not.

The hippy along with his hurt because of the premature interruption drove off further into downtown; Denis and the student got off. He lit a cigarette on the last step of the bus and looked around the stop while buttoning his jacket. Was she there? Just as he was deciding quite disappointedly that he was going to the concert alone, Mary stepped into the light of a street lamp from the darkest corner of the stop, from beneath a tree growing, as it were, straight out of the asphalt.

'So, where is this church of yours?' she continued his metaphor, though she knew where they were actually going. When that morning their conversation again safely sank beneath the roar of the bus engine, Denis put one of his Walkman earphones to her ear and explained that it was a concert and she really had to see the band. Leaving the stop, he offered her a hand, but she didn't take it. She put both hands in her pockets to warm them, and he did the same. Although there were still quite a few people outside the hall, you could hear the concert had already begun. He again saw the student from the bus on the steps by the entrance: of course, she had been on her way here. Most of the band's fans were probably female university students who cared about things. Mary seemed impressed by the impressive stairway adorned with large stone columns and sculptures rising towards the hall entrance; it looked more like a museum or opera house entrance than an entrance to a rock venue. The stairway conveyed the image of a dim passage between two worlds in counterpoint to the somewhat mournful and melancholy rock 'n roll pouring down on them. She slowed her steps a little, as if suspecting that when she crossed over and entered the hall the needle on her compass would completely change the direction it had steadily held for all those years; Denis had to wait at the top of the stairway for a moment or two for her to overcome her hesitation and move on. Just at that point, the opening riff of a song Denis immediately recognized reached the high ceiling. The instrument sobbed as if the guitarist was choking it. 'Let's get closer to the stage!' he yelled, grabbing Mary by the hand, and making his way through the swaying bodies. They stopped somewhere in the middle, where they could clearly make out the figures on stage. Her eyes fixed on the woman at the keyboard.

'That's Margita! Once she was a piano prodigy, but on the way to the conservatory in Russia she joined a rock band!' he yelled in her ear.

'She chose freedom over people's expectations.'

He sensed how the woman on stage, and especially her story, which Denis had telegraphed to her in hollers, captivated Mary. She didn't take her eyes off of her for even a second. He noticed an uncanny similarity between them.

'What's the song about?' It was Mary's turn to yell in his ear.

He stepped behind her. With his left hand he moved her long hair from her ear. It slipped through his fingers for an endlessly long time. Then he took her by both hands and translated the words into her ear.

'The shine in our eyes is deep and unreal, we're travelling in words and thinking in steps, you and me, you and meeee! Stand by me, stand by me…'

He sensed how the words he was sending into her ear shot through her body and reverberated in her finger tips, intertwined with his. The charm ended with the final beat of the song. She dropped his hands, turned, said, 'I'm sorry', and started making her way through the crowd to the exit. He went after her, although he in fact didn't intend to stop her. When she got out of the hall, she ran off into the fog. He ran after her a few steps, then stopped, said, 'Damn it!' and turned back to the hall. Mary the escaped Mormon was all that interested him from that point on, even though the Berlin Wall was already in ruins, students lay dead on Tiananmen Square, and the east of his country was in threatening convulsions.

# MARY

Mary walked around the flat again, observing the emptiness he had left behind. Most of the things were still here; he hadn't taken much with him: his clothes, quite a few books, disks, and records – nothing of the sort that would be sorely missed and provide a loud reminder of his departure. She agreed with it and contributed a good deal to it, but she nonetheless feared the parting moment. It had been a long time since she was last alone. If it still seemed to her a month or so ago that they were constantly in each other's way, depriving each other of air, that if one of them didn't halt the downward spiral they would be at each other's throats, she was now asking herself whether they had really tried everything and perhaps had thrown in the towel too quickly. As he was leaving, he carefully packed paperback copies of Kerouac, Roth, and Auster into his suitcase… he had patiently built his collection over the last few years, finding the books exclusively in small, barely surviving bookstores. He had already read them all, and she could hardly believe he would pick them up again. On the other hand, he didn't take any of the photo albums from their trips. That hurt. As if he was afraid the photos, in which they were almost without exception happy, would shake his resolve to leave. Those frozen moments of happiness taken in different parts of the USA were now all hers, to instil in her nostalgia and doubts. Despite their plans, they never made it to Europe. Not together.

A photo taken on a trip to California two years ago came to mind. They were standing in an embrace on the large, dark rocks under the Golden Gate Bridge. A young surfer in a wet suit of whom they had asked the favour just a second before he waded into the very uninviting sea bloated with waves, had pressed the shutter the instant Mary was trying to tame her long hair, which the strong bay wind had tousled like bunches of unmown grass. She had just managed to remove them from her face, allowing the picture to capture her smile, which had always attracted male as well as female attention. Lately, looking at the photo, she would often wonder how their relationship could have gone downhill so quickly that they weren't able to seize on it and save it, although they both certainly believed it was worth it. That windy day in San Francisco they went to visit the Haight-Ashbury neighbourhood, which was the heart of the hippy world at the end of the 1960s. They walked uphill under a thick net of tangled trolley wires past the colourful facades of townhouses and tried to catch traces of the summer of love that after forty years might not yet have completely gone cold. They found a bit with a street guitarist who was playing all the hits you would expect from the time with the silent accompaniment of an aged Afghan wolfhound stretched out in true hippy style next to an open guitar case. Mary was moved by nostalgia, despite the fact that she had not even been born when these hills teemed with colourful hippies. They stood at the small street concert long enough to hear Janis and her 'Bobby McGee' and Scott McKenzie with flowers in his hair. Then, after throwing a few coins in the open case, for which they got a casual wink from the guitarist, they headed back to the hotel. After a few beers in the hotel bar and a joint at their room window, they made love long into the night before falling asleep in an embrace, exhausted and perspiring from successive climaxes.

'So, I guess this is it,' said Mary.

'Yeah, I guess so,' he said.

And that was that. She closed the door and was left alone. A month before she had turned forty. There was a totally failed attempt to celebrate, which was the final, plain-as-day sign of their sinking relationship. Today was evidently the first day of her life's second half. She pulled a pack of cigarettes out of her handbag, but a touch told her it was empty. She ran her index finger through it to make sure, then let out a loud 'shit', crumpled the empty pack, and threw it on the table, only a small part of which served for eating. Carefully stacked issues of the *New Yorker* and other magazines, a lot of envelopes that had clearly been opened without a knife, and two books of Leonard Cohen's poetry covered at least half the table. She would have paged through one of the two had she found, instead of emptiness, a cigarette in the pack, and lit it. Most people enjoy a cup of coffee or tea with a cigarette. But Mary usually enjoyed a poem or two by Cohen with her dose of smoke and nicotine. She always read poetry her own way, without making pencil scratches between the lines, without searching for the meaning of individual verses. She simply let herself go to the rhythm and mood of a poem, as if listening to Wes Montgomery's smooth jazz, while the ciga-rette burned down. Since she was missing those several minutes of Zen that she so needed after the farewell at the door, being without cigarettes sent her thoughts in a completely unexpected direction.

Just as the small paper clump of the crumpled Lucky Strike pack rolled towards the edge of the table and then down to the floor, so too did a door, closed for many years somewhere in the attic of her memory, slowly open, and from the dusty vault of the past released certain long forgotten pictures. Pictures of her missionary year in Europe when she was barely seventeen, in a country that not long after her departure (preceded by a series of almost unbelievable events) exploded and blew to pieces. Like the majority of teenagers and adults in Mormon families, she had decided to spend a year in one of the missions the church had founded around the world.

Unlike some of her relatives and friends, she didn't decide to go on a one-year mission out of a desire to convert people or out of charity, which are supposed to be missionaries' two fundamental aims. No. Her two motives were much more secular: to travel and gain experience. To live. Her mother tried to convince her to delay leaving for at least a year, but she didn't want to heed her mother's warnings that missionary work was hard and that you have to follow very strict rules that permit little free time. She could hardly wait to get on the plane that would take her over Utah's high mountains and across the Atlantic to Europe, which she dreamed of as some sort of wonderland; an amusement park in which adventures and experiences would follow in such a wild rhythm that she would barely be able to deal with it. When she dreamed of Europe, she naturally dreamed of fields of lavender in Provence, Ireland's green coast, hidden beaches on the Greek islands, Paris coffeehouses, and London pubs. She first heard of Ljubljana, a city in a country with the difficult-to-pronounce name of Yugoslavia and supposedly only several hours by car from Vienna and Venice on the evening of a large meeting of future missionaries, where they told her the location of her mission. She and Noah, the son of family friends of similar age, together with three other missionaries, were to try and start a mission under the supervision of an established Austrian one in the neighbouring socialist country. Since she knew nothing at all about Ljubljana, she couldn't really be disappointed. Nonetheless, she somehow envied Vondra, who was setting off for Lisbon. Lisbon… Lisbon sounded a lot more colourful and fun. That evening Mary's parents bent over a map of Europe and put their heads together. In her room just before falling asleep, Mary heard her father's worried conclusion that his daughter was going to live with communists.

More than fifteen years must have passed since she last thought of him. Denis – what could have happened to him? Had he been swallowed up in the fire of war? Fortunately, the war had not lasted long in that westernmost part of Yugoslavia, only a few days, and as she recalled, his father was a member of the Federal Army, which had to withdraw south from there very soon after. Had Denis stayed in music, or had he grown up and found some serious job? She could hardly imagine the latter; the seventeen-year-old she last saw in a Ljubljana police station was still before her eyes. He was straining to look back at her, while the two detectives pulled him in the other direction. It was a scene that hardly predicted an illustrious, if any, career in the civil service or large company. She couldn't remember his last name. She wasn't even sure he had told her. Yeah, if she knew it, she might catch up with him now, Google him, or search for him on Facebook. But at the time his last name seemed to her an unimportant piece of information.

Her head full of dusty memories, the walk to the closest shop for cigarettes and back to the one-room flat passed without her noticing. It was the time of year in New York when the cold could really be miserable. When she closed the flat door behind her, took off the woollen cap, coat and scarf, and leather Canadian boots with leather soles, she opened the fresh pack of cigarettes, took one out (the first one is always hardest to extract), went to the stove (not really wanting to look for a lighter), and with a practised move lit the cigarette from the gas, having moved her long dark hair to the safe side of her neck with the other hand. As she moved it away from the flame – actually just for a second, but even so – several grey hairs showed in the dead light of a dull, classic light bulb. She didn't do much with them even the first time she noticed. She accepted them as a fact she couldn't much control. Finally holding the lit cigarette, she visibly calmed down and took another, very slow walk around the flat, as if wanting to be sure that he really had left and she was still alone. On the way she grabbed the laptop, put it on the kitchen table, sat down, moved the ashtray closer, and put down the cigarette. Then, both hands on the keyboard, she started entering different search words. The search 'Denis from Ljubljana' didn't yield encouraging results: a link to flight schedules between Ljubljana and Saint-Denis and the website of some escort agency that offered a date with an attractive Denise from Ljubljana. Things like that, nothing solid. Of course, neither could Mary recall, in fact she never knew, the last names of Denis's two friends in the band. It was as if all of it had taken place two hundred, and not twenty, years ago. If it had taken place now, they would have exchanged mobile numbers on the first evening, the night of their first date they would have become Facebook friends, and a firm connection would have been established that almost nothing could interrupt, no matter how far from Ljubljana her Mormon group director would have sent her after the newsstand thing. As it was, they moved her a few hundred kilometres away, to a small city in Austria, and contact was lost forever. Denis wasn't her first love, but he was somehow almost her first beloved. A lot of things happened with him for the first time, irreversibly awakening desire in her young body, although they never went all the way. From the first touch of their hands at some local band's concert and whispering verses in each other's ears…

'Hey, wait!' she caught herself on that thought. 'What was the name of that band. C'mon, Mary, try to remember. Russian queen or something… Anastasia? No, no, no… What was it? Fuck!'

She dug the fingers of her right hand into her hair and steadily drummed the table with those on her left. She took the cigarette from the ashtray, inhaled long and strong, put it down, and again drummed the table…

'Catherine, Catherine the Great! Yes! That was the band's name!'

When she excitedly searched 'Catherine the Great' in Google, all of the results were connected with sites that actually had to do with the eighteenth-century Russian ruler; not a trace of any rock band. In the next search she added 'rock band' and bingo!

Wikipedia result:

*Ekaterina velika* (English: Catherine the Great, initially called Katarina II).

'That must be it! Alternative rock, years 1987–1991, yes, that's definitely it!'

A click on the result.

**Ekaterina Velika** (Serbian Cyrillic Екатерина Велика, English: Catherine the Great), sometimes referred to as EKV for short, was a Serbian and former Yugoslav rock band from Belgrade, being one of the most successful and influential music acts out of former Yugoslavia. Initially called **Katarina II** (Serbian Cyrillic Катарина II, English: Catherine II), the band had built up a devoted following that greatly intensified and expanded after the death of its frontman Milan Mladenović in 1994, which resulted in the dissolution of the band. The group's core consisted of singer and guitarist Milan Mladenović, keyboardist Margita Stefanović and bassist Bojan Pečar, with other members mostly remaining for comparatively shorter periods.

At the side was a black and white photograph of the band.

She, the young woman on the keyboard, and three young men. Just as she remained in her memory. It says she's Margita; it also says she died. Actually, three of the four in the photo were dead. This fact unpleasantly surprised her. Three of the four people who that evening in Ljubljana so assuredly sent their pure, youthful energy into the crowd below the stage were no longer alive. Just like then, at the concert, she now directed most of her attention to the female member as she looked at the band's photo. Even now, something in the young woman greatly attracted her. Maybe the story of how she turned off the road from classical music that others had planned for her. Maybe she was just attracted by the idea of a dark, gentle woman (at this age, she too fit that description) in an alternative rock band made up of men.

Evening fell as she was watching recordings of the band on YouTube. The street lights came on, snowflakes started drifting from the sky, and at a twentieth-floor window of a red Brooklyn building the silhouette of a slender, long-haired woman not looking out the window at the street but across the Atlantic and twenty years into the past, at old recordings she never had time to organize either chronologically or by topic. And so they appeared before her eyes that night with no logic to the successive scenes, as if she were opening some short video files that had been lying in the archives of her recorder for years.

**Recording 1**

It's hard to run across a macadam parking lot at night in heels and a long skirt. An ankle twists at almost every step. Despite this, she keeps going, because she heard him run after her, and the loud rhythms of the concert were still coming out of the hall into the foggy street. She doesn't want him to catch her, least of all does she want to fall like some weak game in deep snow, so she tries to run even faster. He doesn't follow for long. She knows he could catch her in just a few steps, but he clearly got the message. She hears his steps slow, how he says 'Damn!' (later she often heard the word because Denis, Peter, and Goran used it almost like a full stop). She still feels his eyes on her back, and she wants to run away as fast as she can. She doesn't know which way to run, because the fog hides all the landmarks, so she decides to go in the direction from which the loudest sound of night-time traffic is coming. When she gets to the main road and the bus stop where she and Denis met, she knows that she'll make it home on foot in less than half an hour, to her room in an old building right by a city park. A worried Noah, who imagines he is her custodian or something, is almost certainly waiting for her. They'll continue the argument from that afternoon, when he unsuccessfully tried to convince her it wasn't wise to go alone on a date with a stranger whom she met by pure chance on a city bus a few hours before. She tried to lend the reasons for her insistence on keeping the date some deeper meaning, citing her missionary calling, although she didn't sound convincing even to herself. Noah threatened that he would have to inform the supervisor if she was really going to stick to her plans, and her parents too, but she was sure he wouldn't actually do that. She knew he liked her too much; he wouldn't want to hurt her. Now, having escaped Denis's embrace and the concert hall, returning on foot through the thick fog, she thinks about how Noah was probably right. It was a bad idea. It's not good to set off on a trip knowing in advance that you won't be able to finish it. All the same, she won't put up with preaching.

When he waits for her at the door to her room, she'll push him away and go to sleep as quickly as possible. And that's what she did, convinced, actually determined that that was all she would have to do with Denis; a little hand holding, some whispering in the ear, and a lot of goosebumps. But he found her the very next day, at the same bus stop where she had got on yesterday. He was sitting with earphones on, reading a little book. He raised his eyes at exactly the right instant to catch the smile she sent him.

### Recording 2

They're sitting in a park beneath the wide crown of an old tree. It's already dark, especially on that bench, because the street lamps don't pierce the branches thick with leaves. The warm spring evening already smells faintly of summer. The distant, steady sound of city traffic is all that intrudes on the almost complete silence. A romantic view on the city illuminated by innumerable lights opens up beneath them. It draws their attention for only a short while, as long as they sit next to each other holding hands. After a few gentle kisses, Mary decisively moves into his arms. Denis's right palm now travels across her side and up towards her breasts, slowly, like the first scout on enemy territory. After each centimetre covered, it stops and checks if the way is clear, then cautiously continues on to the next piece of untouched skin that with every breath moves away from his palm for a second before immediately returning to its firm grip with the next. Denis's left hand occupies the forbidden territory of her smooth right hip, and the closer it is to its goal, that gentle curve where her leg rounds into her ass, the more pronounced the goosebumps rising under the pillows of his cautious fingers. Exhilaration, a slight twinge, and Mary's ever slower and deeper breathing excites his; he presses his face closer, they wrestle more, taking turns nipping mouth, tongue, and neck. He feels a hardening; they're both a little embarrassed. He tries to move off a little, but she pretends she doesn't notice. When after slow, centimetre moves he finally reaches his goal and touches her breasts for the first time, they quickly retreat and hide, as if frightened off. As if she didn't know what his palm is coming for. It, too, jumps away because of her reaction. She sighs and takes him by the hand. He slowly withdraws his palm from her grip and again occupies the same place, smiling and whispering some words in his language before again burying his head in her neck. When she takes his hand once more to remove it from an excited nipple, her grip has no strength. Her reserve, which church, school, and parents had built up over all those years, crumbled almost without a fight, and her passion burst forth so powerfully that it surprised them both.

# PETER & GORAN

A night-time telephone ring that harshly rouses a man from his dreams, with no compassion, always triggering fear. Fear of the news it brings, waiting in the phone for us to release it with the touch of a green button. There's seldom good news at night; it is more patient and waits for morning, which seems too distant for bad and unexpected news. It has to get out right away. Peter's mobile phone rang at the time of night when not one window in the whole neighbourhood was lit. Only the tightly spaced street lights. At that dead hour of night, they actually shine for no one. As if they were only there to declare this is city, not countryside. City people let thousands of such street lights and countless lanterns of various kinds burn even when they sleep, as if afraid of that genuine black night. You have to go past the city limits, to the countryside, where people always turn the lights out before bed, to experience a true, thickly woven dark night.

The neighbourhood where at flat 16, fifteenth floor, windows still dark, the mobile rang and roused Peter from his sleep, consisted of something more than thirty buildings. The lowest ones were only five stories, the highest ones up to twenty-five. All together they formed a unified terrain of iron and concrete. It was built in the early 1970s between three smallish villages on the edge of the city. When you exited the concrete terrain down concrete steps as if exiting some airliner or ship, you instantly found yourself with two feet planted in the countryside, without any fluid transition. You were suddenly no longer in the city but in a small, unspoiled

Slovene village – houses with tidy balconies, a butcher, volunteer fire department, little church, and a small, almost full cemetery in which the last free spaces still await the very oldest members of the community, people who have been there since the city was still about an hour away on foot and who haven't yet accepted the fact that at a certain moment, when they weren't paying enough attention, it might creep right up to their village. Viewed from a distance, the neighbourhood looked like a huge spaceship that landed among the peacefully sleeping villagers like some Galactica, with innumerable small lights, and docked there for an undetermined time. It forever ended their flawlessly black nights and brought with it strange speaking beings from other planets who on the weekends at first cautiously, then more loudly and in larger groups, set out on exploratory hikes through their village and farther, into their fields and gardens, all the way to the Sava river and back.

The polyphonic melody of a recent hit Peter had loaded on his mobile didn't immediately call him to a waking state, as some old alarm clock would undoubtedly have done. Each time he almost woke up and passed for a split second from sleep to reality, he fell asleep the next second; this was repeated several times until he forced himself to come to. The red numbers 3 and 25, separated by a colon, were flashing before his eyes. The first few seconds he couldn't decipher their meaning. Ah, it's time, the alarm, he thought. He hit the off button a few times, but the repeating melody kept piercing his ears like a long, thin drill straight to his brain. 'Damn… the phone!' After having wandered separately for a few seconds through his drugged consciousness, the fact that it was actually his phone ringing and the fact that it was only a little before 3:30 in the morning collided, and the collision caused a minor explosion of fear that spread first from his head to his rib cage and then to all his limbs, causing them to shake hard.

A forty-year-old, middle rank, office worker in the Ministry of Culture, Peter's previous workday evening had ended almost the same way as all the other evenings of all the other workdays the past two months. On the way back from work – he went on foot now – he stopped in a bar where everyone knew him, drank two beers, ate a hot sandwich, then on the way home smoked three ultralight Wests and at the building entrance exchanged some pleasantries with a neighbour from the sixth floor who happened to be walking her Highland Terrier. She got in a conversation with him only to find out whether his divorce was final. When he confirmed that, she expressed surprise and sympathy. During the conversation, he decided that her bottom was really a little too large and her full breasts were slowly losing the battle against gravity, but that despite this he would gladly have at them if she offered him the chance. In parting he also invited her to stop for a cup of coffee sometime. Then, while getting in the lift, he once again saw his bald spot was growing and said, 'Fuck, everything's going to hell,' and finally in his flat, while still in his ugly but practical windbreaker, hurled himself on the couch, picked up the remote, and turned on the sports channel, which was showing a league match. Two unfamiliar teams with difficult to pronounce names played for him, while at the bottom of the screen current results of all kinds of other matches scrolled by. He slowly dug crumpled bets he made yesterday out of a pocket in his windbreaker to see if he might have hit on any of his wagers. Already on the first two pairings his selections turned out wrong, so he didn't bother to check further. He resignedly crumpled up the paper and instead of putting it in the bin, which was too far from where he was sprawled on the couch, he stuck it back in his pocket. It was obvious that the chances of him someday hitting the sports lottery were as good as him managing to get some decent sex in the foreseeable future. The last time, with Nataša from the finance office, was too great a catastrophe to really count. He tired of the fifty-year-old, whose husband had left her for someone twenty years younger, after five minutes of sex without foreplay, with her screaming and calling endlessly on everyone from God to her mother.

He rolled out of bed as the ringing became louder – something that was not that simple on account of the extra kilos he had progressively gained over the past fifteen years. For a few seconds he couldn't actually locate the phone. He finally found it between three empty cans that he had left on an end table by the television the night before. He could allow himself such a mess after Tanja and the child had left. While he was looking for the phone, he was seized with fear that something had happened to little Luka. Soon after his birth, Peter became acquainted with a whole variety of fearful nuances that he hadn't known before. Sometimes he would have an irrational attack of fear that something would happen to the little one. Then he was afraid something was wrong with him, or that Tanja would be a victim in some way. He never ever talked with anyone about these fears, because he understood them to be weaknesses, which he didn't want to reveal. But when it seemed to Peter that his phantom impending catastrophes were going too far, he was able to comfort himself: they were only the first signs of a midlife crisis, and he would have to get used to them.

When he finally turned up the phone and read Goran's name on the screen, he first breathed out and then sat down on the couch. He sensed the fear slowly receding, and anger taking its place. He had known Goran his whole life, so to speak. They grew up together on the North Side, where their parents had moved right after it was built. Goran was one of those people that you can't remember first noticing or meeting. Goran was simply always there. All of Peter's childhood memories were full of him. He was at all the birthday parties and in the school pictures. From pimply kids with yellow kerchiefs in the first photograph they turned into teenagers in jeans and heads covered with hair gel. The last one was taken at graduation in the school cafeteria, outfitted like a kind of dance hall for the occasion. They gradually lost touch somewhere between their thirtieth and thirty-fifth birthdays, when Peter got married, something that ended ingloriously not long ago, while Goran continued his bachelor life as a manager in a small factory. During the first year after the wedding, when Luka was born, Goran might call twice a week at similar night-time hours from his outings to bars and, drunk on whiskey and sometimes high on cocaine, explain all that Peter was missing while he was folding nappies. When one night Tanja boiled over and told him never to phone at such an hour again, the calls stopped.

'What, don't you have a clock on your fucking Blackberry?' he answered this time, clearly unhappy about the late hour.

'Heh, sorry, man, I'm, hmm, it'll sound strange…'

This time Goran's voice was different, and there wasn't a loud mix of blaring music, clinking glasses, and numerous casual conversations. This time there was complete, pure silence in the background.

'I can't quite figure out, I, screw it... how to… OK, I'll just say it: I'm in a tight corner and can't get out.'

'Where? Fuck! I know that. You don't have to call me at this hour to tell me that.'

'I'm not screwed like that! I'm in a suitcase, briefcase, in a fucking Samsonite! The workers lost the plot, they ran up to the offices, started raising a stink, where's the money, and so on. I thought they were going to lynch me. I shit myself I didn't know what to do, so I hid in a suitcase.'

More than the absurdity of what Goran was telling him, Peter was surprised at how quickly he took on the bizarre story as true. Actually, the whole thing seemed somehow unbelievable, but he didn't long doubt the truth that his childhood friend was calling from his polyurethane business suitcase. While he was listening to Goran's story, he started seeing the outline of events that supposedly took place that afternoon in a small factory at the edge of town, and a faint smile started playing over his face.

That morning, Goran was bargaining on his office phone with one of his clients for him not to send payment for a job to the company's account, because the voracious government was waiting for it along with perpetually dissatisfied employees and a lot of lenders, but to send it instead to the account that he and the director, Stepinšek had quietly opened at a Liechtenstein bank, when he heard the security guard yelling downstairs, followed by the approaching pounding of many pairs of heavy work boots doggedly coming up the stairs. Fortunately, they went past Goran's office and to Stepinšek's first.

Jože Stepinšek had been the director of the insulation materials company for more than twenty years. During that time, he had risen, by means of some clever moves, from ordinary socialist director of a state-owned enterprise all the way to majority owner. He hired Goran as an intern as soon as the latter graduated from the School of Economics, at the request of his father, who during his years as an inspector often did audits at the company. Of course, the audits always ended up in Stepinšek's office over exceptional single malt, expertly served in exquisite glasses shaped like tulips. And of course, Goran's father, his tongue and throat soothed by the rich Lagavulin taste, had no thought of entering any of the blatant violations in his report. Stepinšek immediately took a liking to Goran because he was young and acted by the book, and soon Goran became his main confidant. The first several years, it went really well for them. The company was getting subcontracts on all of the largest projects in the country, and like a rising river, money filled its account and spilled over its banks. It was naturally Stepinšek who enjoyed the greatest share of the good years' fruits. First, he built a huge villa on the edge of Ljubljana and then vacation houses on the coast and in the mountains. But old Stepinšek also allotted a respectable share of the success, which he measured exclusively by the number of zeroes on any given invoice, to his young protégé. Goran bought himself a modest penthouse downtown, which he turned into the debauched bachelor's pad of his wettest youthful dreams. He parked his Mercedes SL 350, a two-seat sports convertible that Peter jokingly called a 'gaymobile' in his reserved spot in the garage under the building. Goran regularly brought women home in it – from those obviously fascinated with his possessions to those Peter would have without hesitation bet half his pay that they couldn't have been taken with such empty invitations, and that they were after something completely different. The latter kept disappointing him when the next day Goran would report all the details of the evening, about every intimate corner of their bodies, every loud gasp, and the dirty words they let out as they neared climax.

After some weighty words from the rebellious workers, Stepinšek, genuinely enraged, raised his voice threateningly, convinced that the world outside his stylishly appointed office was still the same as he saw it when he came in that morning. Neither at that moment did Goran think too much of the commotion in the hall. He assumed that old man Stepinšek would handle the ingrates, say a few powerful words about loyalty, and chase them back to work. Up until now, the men in blue smocks and overalls would always return each to his own machine, turn them on without a word, and continue where they had left off – not satisfied, that is, but reconciled to the facts as laid out in Stepinšek's sermon. The subdued hum of the machines again drowned out the music coming from the old transistor in the corner of the production room, and somewhere aloft in the atmosphere, blending in harmony with the clacking of the money counter's motor that Goran heard every other week in the Liechtenstein bank's vault, there played a hymn to him: to Stepinšek and other victors throughout history. That's how things always fell into place.

But this time, the world in which gloomy men in blue smocks and overalls cast their eyes down and acquiesce when old man Stepinšek raises his voice, disappeared sometime between the start of the workday and lunch. When Stepinšek's thundering at the rebellious men peaked, just when he was effectively to conclude his sermon, from somewhere, completely unexpectedly, totally out of the context of the established rules, as if in slow motion, there came a slap that changed everything. Goran heard it just at the door to his office, wanting to go out into the hall to see yet another of Stepinšek's triumphant finales, after which the defeated troop of men in blue go back downstairs. The blow from a large, heavy, cold-swollen hand against the old director's still soft cheek had a mighty, almost exaggerated sound effect. As if someone slammed the cymbals with all his might at the end of a wild rock 'n roll piece, the sound of the slap marked the moment when some irretrievable old era came to an end, one in which roles were clear and assumed by everyone present, and there was a transition to something new, and none of those present had the slightest idea what was coming, and no one understood how it would work out. Goran's immediate instinct was to lock himself in his office, move away from the door, and circle the space nervously two or three times. Then he again approached the door and tried to make out what was happening in Stepinšek's office. For a few seconds after the slap exploded, nothing at all could be heard. Just a menacing silence. He imagined the surprised looks on the faces of the shocked director and workers, who were probably somewhat terrified at their own actions. But only for a short time. When the minutes of fear and disbelief passed, the hinges finally came off. Blows started raining down on Stepinšek. None of them reached the sound effect of the first, historic slap, probably because the director hid his face in his palms, crossed over his face. The blows now sounded duller, because they were falling on the sleeves of his cotton jacket. They gradually increased, like a hailstorm preceded by one fat advance pellet. After several seconds of quiet, another falls, then a third and a fourth, and they increase mightily until the climax, and… silence again. The last blow could be heard after a short pause interrupted only by Stepinšek's quiet groaning and the secretary Suzi's somewhat hysterical sobbing. Goran then clearly heard a kick. The guy must have aimed it more at the parquet floor than at Stepinšek's crotch, because you could hear his sole hit the floor, and the dull blow of his toe against the ball of the director's curled up body was barely audible. Apparently at least one of the enraged workers took pity on the old director, had a hard time deciding to hit him, was almost too late, but in the end did give him a toned down one so as not to stand out from the incensed mob.

'I knew they'd come for me next, but I couldn't think how to get away. I could only get the fuck out the window and bust my… So I quickly started to make myself small, so small that I could close the suitcase. Now I can't get out, the workers took over the whole factory, they're in Stepinšek's office drinking his single malt like it's lemonade, the tossers, and they're screaming at Stepinšek: 'Go get the money you hid, you old pig!' and so on. They're taunting the poor secretary, Suzi, and grabbing her ass. You can't believe it.'

'So the guys in blue lost it, bravo' Peter thought to himself. He was surprised at the malice he felt listening to his shaken and reduced friend, but he couldn't help himself. He felt some perverse satisfaction, as if universal Justice had been done that morning in the small factory at the edge of town. He could only hope – he couldn't be sure – that the sweetish feeling of satisfaction that crept into his voice even as he unsuccessfully tried to hide it was the result of his inborn sense of justice, not something more base, such as envy, which could have seized him in recent years due to the fact that he had been side-lined, shunted into some middling place in the bureaucratic pyramid, where an upward move was unattainable, and a downward one practically impossible, while not only Goran, but others too, even other more or less close acquaintances raced by him on the highway of success, decked out with all of its unmistakable attributes. He never drove that road. He explained to others that not taking part in the race was part of his unbending moral code, but if he were fully sincere, he would admit that for all those years he didn't quite know how to even get on the road. Goran's voice, now quieter and calmer, woke him from this brief contemplation.

'Do you ever think of him? Of Denis?'

As if he sensed through the connection that he and his childhood friend were losing their shared frequency, Goran transported him some twenty years back with the sudden change of topic. The war had ended in time for them to enter the university without problems: Goran to study economics, Peter in the liberal arts, and Denis to art school. By then, not much was left of the long summer between the end of high school and the beginning of their studies. Who would have believed only two years previously that it would be possible to say something as bizarre as 'the war had taken up the first half'. They wanted to spend the second half wandering the Adriatic coast, but they soon realized it wasn't the same there as a year ago. From today's vantage point, the war had hardly even started, but at the time it seemed it had exceeded all reasonable bounds, and its spirit would soon be squeezed back into the bottle, because of course it was clear to Both Sides that it was senseless, while it was everywhere, although at that moment still at a distance, beyond the Velebit, Dinara, and Biokovo highlands. The smell of war overcame the smells of pine trees, the sea, and girls' skin. The echo of its drums brought new songs to the seaside terraces, ones to which you didn't dance, as in past years, in a dim light, your eyes fixed on your partner's eyes and her mysterious smile, across which a light breeze cast her unruly hair, but with arms raised high and eyes fixed on the sky, in a trance, showing your newly discovered allegiance to your tribe and menacing the other. Ritualistic dances replaced couples' dances. That wasn't what they had come for, so they returned home early to Ljubljana, in time to avoid starting to believe that at a moment when history was being made and nations were being made it was untoward to look for something as frivolous as summer fun and a little love. Home to Ljubljana! They couldn't know at the time that the same, *their* Ljubljana would a year later mercilessly reject one of them, like a mountain rejects a climber who makes a small but fatal mistake on his ascent.

'Why are you asking me that now?'

There was annoyance, almost anger in Peter's voice at Goran's question.

'Is that a knock on my bad conscience? Don't bother, because I don't have one. What happened to him isn't our fault.'

'I know, I know we're not guilty man, only damn: we didn't do anything to stop it. We let the pigs take him away like a common criminal. We just stood there like two morons.'

A late autumn day in 1992. They were just leaving classes.

At first, Goran and he practised alone in the bunker of Peter's building for several months. Peter played guitar and Goran drums. Denis joined them a little later, not long before getting involved with that American, because the minimum number for a rock band is three, not two. He brought a bass guitar he bought through an ad. But not because he had some special liking for the instrument: it was simply the only opening in the band that didn't yet exist. And vocals. Denis was a very ordinary bassist but an extraordinary singer. His somewhat cracking voice lent colour to their band, which otherwise didn't differ from similar garage bands with ordinary musicians and lousy sound – a lot of noise with some rhythm and maybe a melody, if you strained to hear it.

They were coming back from classes that late autumn day. Evening had already come on when they were crossing the Three Bridges in the middle of a heated debate about music, and two policemen – one large, almost huge; the other small, almost a midget – stopped them and demanded their papers. The red-faced, jovial giant inspected Peter and Goran's ID cards, while the midget, obviously the meaner half of the grotesque pair decided to mess with Denis.

'I don't have any, but I've got a driver's license.'

'What do you mean you don't have any?'

'Well, I don't. But all the information is here on the driver's license, address, ID number, everything.'

'Wait here, and I'll check.'

The uniformed midget took Denis's driver's license and winked at the giant. They both stepped aside and started talking over the radio with someone who was obviously at the police station. Ten metres away, Peter, Goran, and Denis resumed their conversation without paying attention to the policemen, who were acting more and more confused. They spread their arms and looked at one another as if they didn't understand the instructions the invisible authority had radioed to them. Having finished the communication, they kept heatedly debating between themselves. The midget slightly bumped into the giant, elucidated something to him, and hit him on the chest with the back of his hand, while the giant used his left hand to raise his cap a number of times so as to scratch his head with his right, like a person who couldn't comprehend the situation he was in. When it was clear the midget had concluded his sermon, they both turned to the young men, who had moved to the closest bench, lit cigarettes, and were even more heatedly debating something clearly unconnected with the policemen's actions. They didn't even notice that the policemen were again approaching them, and that the midget pulled his cap lower to make a more authoritative impression. His unbearably high voice interrupted the three friends' conversation.

'Denis, sir, you are in Slovenia illegally. You don't have a valid residence permit.'

'Huh?' All three turned in the direction from which the repugnant voice was coming. Then Peter and Goran looked at Denis questioningly.

'Who's here illegally? I've been here forever, for sure I was in Ljubljana long before YOU drove in from the provinces.'

While the large policeman took a jab in the background at his smaller colleague's Styrian accent, the latter's face first turned violet, and then he grabbed Denis by the left elbow.

'Up, we're goin' to the station, we'll tell you about it there nice and slow.'

Denis pulled his clutched arm and tried to wrench it out of the policeman's grasp, so the latter seized the collar of his olive-green jacket with the other hand and pushed him in the opposite direction.

'OK, OK, OK. I'm coming! Peter, just take please my bass so THESE IDIOTS don't wreck it for me.'

'But what's wrong, where are you taking him? Don't you have anything better to do?'

'You two just watch out for yourselves, we'll lay it all out for Mr. Denis at the station.'

And they were gone. Peter and Goran stood and watched the three leave the Prešeren Square for the police station on Trdin street: the quick midget policeman on the left, the jovial giant on the right, and Denis in the middle, his hands stuck in his jeans pockets, his head hanging between his shoulders, and his field jacket collar raised. They didn't even say good-bye, there wasn't even a friendly hand slap, and Denis didn't once look back once. They didn't know it, but he was leaving their lives forever. He wasn't going off into the sunset, because the sun had already set on the left, and it wasn't a happy ending. He was marching off into the increasingly cold gloom of an autumn evening with the two policemen.

'Screw it, what could we have done? Fight with the pigs and save him or what? You know that after we called all over, what's with him, but not one person could tell us what to do.'

'I don't know, man, don't know what, I only know when I think of us standing there on Prešeren Square like two idiots, just looking at them taking him away, I get sick. I feel like some Kraut by some 'factory' that smoked and stank for four years but never figured to ask, Mother fuck, what is that stink?'

'Cut it out. Now you're going to lay some pain on me from that Samsonite case of yours. After all we tried, you know I went to Uncle Stane and told him to screw himself. Don't know what else I could've done…'

Peter's Uncle Stane, his mum Alenka's brother, the son of the high party functionary Janez, looked at his nephew across his office desk on one of the floors of the Internal Affairs Ministry building that winter afternoon. On his desk was a miniature gilded pole on a marble pedestal from which hung a small Slovene flag. At that moment it seemed quite bizarre to Peter, although it was not at all an unusual decoration in official offices. He imagined how microscopically small animals for whom the table was the main square of a country bordered by the walls of Uncle Stane's office line up every morning and salute it. ('The little country is small but it's all ours', they probably rub their little feet together.) Books were stacked on two shelves in a glass case over Uncle Stane's shoulder. The ones on top were supposed to impress the visitor with the importance of his position and the duties he carried out: the constitution, laws, reference works, a very fat book on human rights, and European and UN conventions. Among the books on the lower shelf that were supposed to make an impression about Stane as an individual was a 1968 monograph (when Stane the student was occupying the college, marching in the streets, and angering his father, a party functionary in the Secretariat for Internal Affairs who gave the national police chief special instructions not to use any force against the young demonstrators, among whom were many sons and daughters of various important people) against which there leaned a collection on the service of police reserve units during the ten-day war. From the wall left of the table, *El Comandante* looked at both Peter, a second-year philosophy student, and Stane, a highly placed official in the Ministry of Internal Affairs, from a black and white poster – an assurance to Peter and everyone else who visited the office that its occupant had not forgotten (or worse, betrayed) his youthful ideals. No, no: The same hot blood flowed through that 47-year-old body in a three-piece suit with a small European flag on the button, that had flowed through it in the glorious year of 1968.

'Listen, Peter, I looked into it. There's nothing to be done in this case. The young man, your friend Denis, wasn't of Slovene nationality, he didn't apply for Slovene citizenship after Slovenia's secession from Yugoslavia and he also didn't register as a foreigner, so consequently, by force of the law, he was erased from the Slovenian register of residents. Practically speaking, he's been living illegally in the country since last year. Anyway, his parents left back in 1991 with the Yugoslav National Army.'

'Uncle Stane, what do you mean foreigner status? After all, he lived his whole life in Ljubljana, in a building on the North Side, three down from us, his mum didn't spit him out yesterday, so why should he ask for permission to live here?'

'Listen, Peter, your friend didn't regularize his status. Nothing more can be done here.'

'But he tried. He went twice to the office on Mačkova street, and every time some woman at the window sent him back for more papers, I was with him. The last time we were there, there was such a fucking mob, and we were late for a concert...'

'Peter, nothing more can be done now.'

'Screw it, in whose name are YOU doing this? Who told you it's cool to throw people out of the country? For nothing?'

'Who, who, what kind of questions are those? Our people decided for their own country, in a referendum.'

'There you have it, our people decided in a referendum. You and your people took a lot from that one question. I was also for it, but I don't remember, maybe I'm mistaken, correct me, that there was something on the ballot like: are you for throwing the bassist and singer of your band – and your friend – the fuck out of the country?'

Peter quickly got up and in so doing bumped the desk with his knee, so that the miniature Slovene flag jumped, flipped, and fell, bounced twice, and lay there motionless. He wasn't able to say anything sensible, he was so enraged, and despairing in the face of his impotence and defeat, he ended the conversation childishly, as if it was a fight with some kid on the street.

'Wellll… Shit on you and your whole 1968, and fuck your Che Guevara!'

Uncle Stane silently watched his nephew leave his office as he put his mini flag back in its place. Three years later, at his sister's request, he would arrange a job for him in the Ministry of Culture.

'And how you think you'll get out of the suitcase? You have some beans handy to munch on or what?'

'Hell how am I to know. All I wanted was to make myself small. I only, wait, wait a minute. Something's going on. There's some hole here… what the hell. Yeah, yeah, now there's some hole at the end of the suitcase… I'll try to crawl out… Damn it's so narrow… OK, I can't with the phone, later, talk to you.'

Beep, beep, beep, beep, beeeeeep.

# DENIS, 1994

Before he went in, he always tried to get as much of the dirt he picked up on the way as he could off his boots. The soil on them was dry, there hadn't been any rain for several weeks, but despite this, at every stomp on the rug quite a bit of soil and dust came off them, and he could never completely clean them. As always, some was left on them right up until the instant he was about to enter. Then in three or four steps, all the filth would spill to the floor by itself, onto the library parquet. He passed the desk where the librarians were supposed to be sitting. There was no one there now, and he went up the stairs to the fiction section. On the third step, he looked back and saw that halfway between the entrance and the stairs he had left some dirty tracks behind. He went back to the desk, took out a worn broom and with careful, exact movements wiped the dusty tracks into a little pile, which he then pushed out the door onto the street. When the parquet was again impeccably clean, he put the broom back and once again headed past the shelves with the social sciences, political science and history, and up the steps to the novels, folk tales and short stories.

He always had trouble with returning books on time and paying fines to libraries. Not infrequently they exceeded the cost of the old, worn books he was returning. Ever since he was small he liked to borrow books, enjoyed choosing them, paging through them, and wasting time between the bookshelves, but he was always too restless for disciplined, regular reading. He would check out much more than he actually read. Three weeks always passed by too quickly, but he delayed returning them since each return of an unread book seemed to him like a small personal defeat, with the result that he would bring them back, most still unread, more or less delinquent, for which he would have to pay. He became a real master of excuses, by which he somewhat reduced the fines. To increase his credibility, he would blame it on his parents, grandparents, neighbours, neighbours' dogs, illnesses, moves, and sometimes even himself.

His love of order in that library without librarians open twenty-four hours a day, seven days a week, was the exact opposite. He wanted to read as much as possible while he was in the town, before they moved again, and before the rain came. The first rain would surely ruin the library's upper floor together with all its fiction and poetry. Every time he went up the stairs, he looked up to the rafters, where the roof that should have been there was gone. Depending on the time he visited, the bookshelves were lit by the morning, midday, afternoon, or evening sun; sometimes, when he enjoyed an evening or night-time visit, by the moon and stars. He had already spent three weeks in the town without residents, with a library missing a roof and librarians. He ironically named it the 'convertible library'. He had already borrowed a dozen books, the last of which especially nicely applied to his story and the situation in which he found himself. He never thought a novel that a year or two before had seemed just burdensome school reading would bring such pleasure not long after graduation. Albert Camus's *The Outsider* didn't stir him anywhere near as much during his school reading as this night, when he read it in one sitting, underlining certain passages. It was obviously required school reading in this town, too, since everywhere there were underscorings and notes. His marks were but the last of many traces the pupils of the town without residents had left before him, when everything was still different, when people were living here, and when he himself was living differently and elsewhere, with people for whom the story of the town and his role in it is now almost a complete blank; perhaps it fills just a small part of the international news in the evening broadcasts. The library's upper floor was illuminated by the evening sun's warm red light, which quietly and softly fell on the bookshelves and caressed the spines of the abandoned books. He walked through an excited multitude of dust particles that danced its evening dance in the departing light shafts to return the book he had just read to the shelf with a capital C and the section marked Ca, to the place marked with a black and white cassette cover. Before he put it in its place, the old book with an ascetic appearance and a soft cover that had often been repaired with tape, called to him one more time. He started paging through it once more, his index finger travelling through the thicket of its tiny type, as if wanting again to run the course of a slowly walked path, making occasional stops at underlined parts of the story, the little places of special reading enjoyment and pondering that he marked that night. He looked over to the shelves with H authors and noticed a red, shabby, retro easy chair, a design achievement of the 1960s or 1970s, from a time when the people living in the town clearly felt the need for beautiful things. It reminded him of the wonderful crystal chandelier that proudly resisted events below, from the ceiling of some living room in Beirut simply by dint of its unwavering presence, while two members of one of the warring militias sent their rounds through a window into the street. In that Beirut scene, framed in his memory by the wooden cabinet of an Iskra colour television, the central point of the living room from his childhood, below which he had quietly to play with plastic cowboys and Indians while the news was on, was a chandelier – a monument to lost normalcy, and a red easy chair just like the one in this library with no roof.

With strong blows, he managed to get some of the dust off the seat and back of the red easy chair, then he removed the bandana he had tied on like a pirate and removed the helmet from the left side of his belt and put it on a shelf. He took the Kalashnikov off his right side over his head, took off his belt and jacket, pulling a pack of *Drinas* and a lighter from his upper left pocket, and finally lay back in the still dusty red chair. As he was looking over the books on the shelf to his right, a thin book on which was written *Hermann Hesse: Siddhartha* caught his eye, and he decided it would be his next read. He knocked on its spine and said, 'You're goin' with me today.' There were still four cigarettes in the soft pack; he stuck one in his mouth, lit it, and again started paging through *The Outsider*. Another advantage of such a library without a roof and staff was definitely that you could light a cigarette at any time and peacefully smoke while paging through a book. His index finger stopped on the first marked page, where a blue fountain pen and before it two different pencils had underlined the text: 'I've often thought that had I been compelled to live in the trunk of a dead tree, with nothing to do but gaze up at the patch of sky just overhead, I'd have become used to it by degrees.' Two more sentences were underlined a little further along: 'There were others in the world worse off than I. I remembered it had been one of mother's pet ideas – she was always voicing it – that in the long run one gets used to anything.' When he had read the underlined text one more time, he put the book down on his thigh and threw his head far back so that he could look straight up into the evening sky above, through the missing roof, and he thought how fucking true that thought was.

If someone had told him a half a year ago, when he was still in Ljubljana and someone completely different, an art school student and a bass player and singer in an unknown band, that in a few months he would be wearing a tribal military uniform and roaming about an empty town that all the members of a rival tribe had fled, he would have laughed. But now he is where he is, and already used to it all. He is used to belonging exclusively to his one tribe, by definition of which the members of other tribes become the enemy. He's used to the uniform, used to the helmet and Kalashnikov, used to the empty villages and towns awaiting them every time they advance, used to not asking and not thinking about why all the villages and towns in their path are like that, and used to the target he constantly feels on his helmet. He's also used to the thought that in one of the houses in one of the coming villages they will have just entered there is a sniper waiting just for him, for his target. He also thought about whether Ljubljana got used to his absence just as quickly, and whether Peter and Goran had already got used to him no longer being part of their story, which certainly didn't end because of him. That was for sure, because he hadn't received any calls, letters, or the like from them. Although he didn't get in touch with them after being taken away at the Three Bridges, so they couldn't have even found him if they wanted to.

'And then a rush of memories went through my mind – memories of a life which was mine no longer,' he read further in the marked parts of the book. 'Warm smells of summer, my favourite streets, the sky at evening, Mary's dresses and her laugh. The futility of what was happening here seemed to take me by the throat…'

Young Denis's two different lives, fuck it, there's a real story for you. The first life: Ljubljana, the North Side, a concrete playground, balls, bunker, guitar, band, high school, concerts, friends, Mary, the loss of Mary, war, end of the war, start at the university, paperwork, the end. The second life: paperwork – the start, police station, court of inquiry, police van, border, arrival at his parents' village, gravel, the war, uniform, rifle, marches, empty villages, empty town, 'convertible library', ellipsis, the end yet unknown, although it can be guessed. Is he afraid of it? The end? Afraid of the sniper waiting for his target?

'And, on a wide view, I could see that it makes little difference whether one dies at the age of thirty [or twenty-one?] or threescore and ten – since, in either case, other men and women will continue living, the world will go on as before.' Damn that Camus, the bastard, he really sticks it to you, he thought, and took the next cigarette out of the pack, lit it with the butt of the other, and closed the book. That was the end of his notes. He leaned back and just smoked. The vault of the library was black now, with a large full moon and innumerable stars.

The dark sky above sparkled with innumerable shiny dots that evening as well, when, backpack on a shoulder and Walkman phones in his ears, he appeared at the door of his grandmother's house, where his parents were staying temporarily after their move. His great grandfather had built the house, a *kovanica*, out of wood and stucco from dried mud a century before, when he returned from WWI. It stood on a dusty, unpaved street that ended at a stream, where he hunted frogs and sometimes fished with the village children during summer holidays. He got to the village late, the unlit street was already dark, and he had to step carefully, walking more and more slowly. One light in the house at the end of a large farmyard shone like an orange square. He stood wavering at the gate. He delayed entering because he knew that his mum would start sobbing when she saw him, unexpected, on the threshold. He had no way of alerting her that he was coming. After being escorted across the border, he slowly hitch-hiked – if one can say that about riding on a tractor tow-bar and on the bed of a creaky TAM truck – travelling like in some road movie the route that he drove with his old man and mum twice a year, listening to a cassette tape of the Novi Fosili that time and again they tirelessly rewound in the cassette player with Dolby stereo stamped on it. He could hardly wait to get by his surprised mum and grandma to the downstairs room that always smelled of fresh sheets and dried quince and collapse on the mattress filled with corn husks next to the old sideboard on which there were little yellowed Panini stickers of Robert Charpetier, Roland Mathes, Tom Woods, and Brazilian basketball standouts that he had put there a good fifteen years ago, at the time of the Montreal Olympics. Just before he entered the yard, he looked into the sky, in which an unusually great number of stars jostled, like here at the library, and thought that the sky was as rich with stars as the unhappy village below was empty and poor.

'Fucking paradox, or something like that,' he said to himself when towards the end of the second cigarette he was already drifting into drowsiness. He again dreamt of Mary. They never talked about anything in the dreams, she always just smiled at him, he probably smiled back at her, but he couldn't see himself in the dreams. They were sitting somewhere in a park, facing the sunset, he facing her, so he could follow the sunset on her face, which at first shone a little too much, even blinding him a little, and then gradually took on warmer colours, down to dark red before the sun went out. The dreams always ended exactly at the instant he tried to take her hand; but not this time, this time they continued. He felt her hand in his, but something was wrong. The hand he took wasn't soft and tiny, as he expected. It was large, coarse, and old…

'Denis, Denis, it's gonna rain!' he heard Serbo-Croatian.

As he was waking, the beautiful Mormon girl's face changed and aged, her dark hair became a grey colour, then began to thin and fall out. Almost all of the teeth fell out of her smile. When he awoke, he was holding the hand of a thin, bald, toothless old man repeating in a madman's high, hysterical voice, 'it's gonna rain, it's gonna rain,' all the while spraying Denis with spittle from the spaces between his teeth as he pronounced each word. When he realized what was happening, he first took a deep, terrified breath, blew out, 'ouch, bastard!' then gave the old man, who had almost crawled right into his face, a good kick in the stomach, causing him to stumble back several metres and land on his back. Denis grabbed the Kalashnikov and aimed it from up close at his chest, pinning his shoulders to the floor with a foot.

'What are you doin' here, you shitty bastard?'

The old man started hysterically hooting even more loudly, 'Ha, ha, ha. Ha, ha, ha, it's gonna rain, Denis, it's gonna rain!'

It was dark in the library. The upper floor where Denis and the old madman were, was illuminated only by the full moon and the stars, and the old man's hysterical laughter gave Denis goosebumps over his whole body.

'Get out, you fucker, get out! I'll kill you, motherfucker, I'll kill you like a rabbit!'

He started feeling unnerved, his trigger finger quivered, but the old man only hooted more loudly and hysterically.

'Easy, Denis, you can't do anything to him anyway'.

A man's voice came from the dark behind his back. He jerked around and aimed the rifle at the voice. A young man his age in civilian clothes, in jeans, emerged from the dark into the moonlight, his arms spread and palms open to him.

'Your rifle is useless, Denis,' he said in Serbo-Croatian. It can't do anything to us, we no longer have anything, see? The town is empty. We're only here to help you.'

'Help with what?'

'With the books. It's going to rain, and the roof is gone. The town will need these books again someday. When this ends, when people return or new ones come… Everyone needs stories, stories have the flavour of life, Denis. We've been watching you for a number of days, how you care for the library, everything you borrow, you return, keeping it clean, orderly, but the rain can't be prevented, so we said, let's go help him.'

Denis slowly became aware of the presence of strangers, while the old man kept laughing hysterically behind his back. Several more silhouettes stepped out of the dark. Another young man and three young women, all in their early twenties, all in civilian clothes. He suddenly understood that it wasn't the appearance of a crazy, toothless old man and a group of five young people in civilian dress here in the library under the stars that was grotesque, but in fact he was grotesque and absurd in his tribe uniform, with a helmet and Kalashnikov that he was still pointing at the young people standing calmly before him, apparently not at all upset. He slowly lowered the barrel to the floor and spread his arms.

'OK. Explain to me how you got here and what you want.'

'We've been in this town, Denis, since time immemorial, we grew up here, so the right question may be why are you here and what are you doing, but let's just leave it there.'

Denis smiled, set his rifle back in the corner, took the second-to-the-last cigarette out of the pack, lit it, and said, 'We all had to leave our towns for some other cities. What's with him?' He gestured towards the toothless old man who had already lifted himself off the floor, stopped hooting, and only kept repeating under his breath, 'it's gonna rain, it's gonna rain.'

'Fear, Denis, fear. He's gone mad from fear. Once he was the director of this library, the most well-read person in town, and the five of us were librarians. Right to the end, to the evening you arrived, when after three days of shelling the roof was destroyed. But it is what it is: it's kind of nice out here under the stars, if it weren't for the fucking rain.'

'Ahhh, it's gonna rain, rain, rain. It's gonna rain, ha, ha, ha.'

'It's all right, it's all right, director, calm down.'

The three young women and the other young man didn't speak, they just observed Denis with their eyes, which were far from friendly. The young women in particular showed clear signs of antipathy. That bothered him, he wasn't used to it. Two were blonde, one of them a little thinner, almost bony, he mostly noticed the other's ample bust, even though she was clearly trying to hide it some beneath a long, wide sweater. The third was a brunette with short hair, dressed in jeans and a shirt, which gave her a kind of boyish appearance, for which she probably never captured those first looks from men. Her distinctly long white neck, around which was fastened a thin gold chain, most attracted Denis's attention. Only after he started to look her over more carefully did he discover in her all that escapes a first glance: the quite large, dark eyes, the large, light lips that, very tightly closed, surely hid a beautiful smile, which he justifiably doubted he would partake of that evening. She noticed him looking at her and confidently met his gaze and held it until he averted it, then she triumphantly turned away, clearly showing him that now, no longer staring at her, he didn't deserve her attention. The other young man was obviously a bookworm, in glasses, a shirt buttoned all the way up, and a jumper on top of that, the complete opposite of the one who had spoken to Denis.

'So, the rain's coming, and something has to be done with these books.'

Denis recalled his thought that the history and political science books on the lower floor probably most deserved to be out in the rain.

'Maybe we'll move the literature to the lower floor in place of the histories and political science, which we'll carry up here to rot, fuck 'em. Because those books are full of bullshit and the past.'

The speaker laughed.

'What do you say, Denis, maybe it is really best to leave them out in the rain.'

'It wasn't books that brought all this to pass, nor did it happen all by itself. It was an earthquake, a flood, fire, snow, and all of this, all this around us was orchestrated, it was all orchestrated by YOU, nothing happened of its own accord.'

She didn't yell, she didn't even talk loudly, but only very sharply and plainly. The brown-haired woman with the beautiful neck pronounced a judgment on Denis in a very calm voice, instantly cooling the inspiration that was just starting to warm him. As she pronounced her judgment, she seemed to him complete. An unknown pain that she had to overcome and the hate she showed him turned her face into the picture of perfection, like a master's final brush-strokes. He was defeated. Completely enchanted, like a believer before a holy image, he stood rooted before her and thought, 'Fuck, how pretty you are', and he knew that at that instant he was seeing one of those rare scenes that make everything else worthwhile. 'Lady Madonna' came to mind. John and Paul must have had in mind just such a strong woman, who gets up even stronger after each of life's blows and is even more beautiful as she awaits the next. He thought that such women are all the good that will be left to this shitty country when all this warring is over. Women who proudly and patiently wait for him and the rest of the young men in uniform to stop their war games, so that they can sweep away the whole mess and all the filth left from their play.

The young man, the speaker, called her Azra and asked her to stop, saying they were there only on account of the library and the books.

'Now let's all go and try to save these books.'

Under the blanket of night, illuminated only by moonlight and starlight, six pairs of hands began the great relocation of literature from the upper to the lower floor of the town library. They used deep wooden drawers to carry the books, filling them in order; from authors beginning with A: Andrić, Auster, Atwood, Asimov, to those beginning with B: Balzac, Baudelaire, Bukowski, Borges, Bulgakov, and so on. With each letter of the alphabet, a multitude of authors and their stories journeyed from the upper floor to the lower. History and political theory books travelled upstairs, in the opposite direction – both recently written for the purpose of realizing the centuries-old dreams of those who supported separate tribes, as well as older ones that praised the institution of some dreams of centuries-old remove that at the time were shared by all the tribes that inhabited these parts. Those six young people – five members of one tribe reinforced by a soldier of the other – made the decision to give preference to stories, all kinds of stories, over various kinds of truth that sometimes contradicted one another. Truths went upstairs to await the rain, and stories went downstairs to safety. It had been a long time since Denis felt good in the company of people.

He communicated with practically no one in the unit into which he had been drafted. In all the villages and towns they moved through the past three weeks, all he did was look for the four AA batteries he needed to get the old Walkman he'd brought with him from Ljubljana running again. He had two cassettes with him, EKV's *Ljubav* and the Beatles, recorded on ninety-minute TDK tape. He tried very hard to keep both of them as safe as possible. After all, he didn't know how much more time he would have to spend with the twenty men with whom he had nothing in common but for the supposed tribal belonging. The cassettes were his last tie to normalcy, to his past life, while roaming strange, unfortunate villages and towns. He hoped that the legend of TDK cassettes' indestructibility was true, that at least the Beatles would last for him until the end of this shit. Before his last batteries went dead, he noticed that the EKV recording was unfortunately going bad, which meant the beginning of its unavoidable end. He knew the sound of a stretched tape, and he knew it was an irreversible process. He had now been without batteries a whole week, and so was experiencing a kind of withdrawal process.

He grabbed both cassettes and the Walkman along with some clothes and threw them in a backpack the morning the police escorted him from criminal court to his flat on the North Side where he was allowed to take the most essential things before the police van took him to the border. He had spent the previous night awake in the police station, with which he was already familiar from the incident with Mary and the newsstand. He shivered; he was afraid. He sensed that it was the start of some absurd story, the course of which he couldn't influence. He'd been living alone in Ljubljana since his parents left with the federal army. They were both employed in the army and had practically no choice. He didn't want to go with them, he couldn't imagine moving to some small town, a *varoš*, down south in the Balkans, so he took advantage of having recently come of age and decided to stay. His mum cried, his father had a blank look and was silent; they didn't much object to his decision given his age, which was just right for the draft. That evening in the parking lot in front of the building, by the Lada Samara stuffed with their lives up to that point, his old man hugged and kissed him and told him to be careful and stay in touch, while neighbours peeked from behind the curtains. He travelled their path in the police van a lot sooner than he expected, a good year later. He stuck in his earphones and listened to all the songs, in order, on the *Ljubav* album over and over the whole way to the border. The tracks, which he had long known by heart, were his therapy from that morning on, a return to normalcy, so he now really needed those fucking AA batteries.

When they were almost done moving the books, he carried a drawer with Azra for the first time; it was full of books by authors beginning with K.

'You sure have a nice name, Azra.'

He didn't even dare take a good look at her after she pronounced her judgment on him. But he felt an inordinate desire to engage in some kind of conversation. He felt small next to her, she seemed three metres tall, at once frightening and attracting. The past half hour he was preparing in his head how to break the ice, searching for the optimal opening sentence to soften her in an instant; in the end he managed to put together that empty, idiotic opening line, surely the worst in the history of male-female conversations. Her reaction was fitting. Cold. She gave him an 'are you joking?' look, and he hurried to correct the impression. Without giving a moment's thought to what he was about to do, he started singing:

'I'm a stranger named Denis
from another time, Azra,
losing my head in love
and dying in love.'

It just burst from him unexpectedly and somewhat altered, the last stanza of the old Bosnian love song that he knew from a rock 'n roll rendition, which on his insistence and despite Goran's great dismay ('Now we're going to play damn folk songs?') they played over an entire afternoon of band practice. The first several attempts were hopeless: even if they somehow managed to get the right tempo in the first few verses, they went a little faster with each succeeding one, so that the last stanza – the one with which he was now trying to defrost icy Azra – was completely unrecognizable. Goran pushed it most, on the drums, probably because he was so unbelievably patient with each repetition.

'Goran, come on, dammit, calm down a little on those kegs of yours, for god's sake. You can't keep pushing and pushing, it's not Deep Purple, dammit. It's a Bosnian love song, *sevdah*, so you gotta take your time. You can't speed it up, you gotta go slow, play easy. Better have a drink, we'll have a beer so you go a little easier.'

And so they had one, smoked one, and slowed it down just enough that the song finally sounded as Denis imagined it when getting ready to rehearse.


His unexpected song unsettled her icy pose barely perceptibly, but surely. She kept straining to make a cold, stern impression, but her defensive walls had been breached. A lot of things were mixed into the stanza (in its original version) he sang. In the old love song, Azra was not a girl at all, but an old Arabian tribe whose members fell sick and died from love, for which members of other tribes considered them irrational softies. Since he'd been drafted, his brothers-in-arms often called Denis a softy, pussy, darky, homo, and the like. Because of this he himself sometimes wished he were rougher, maybe then he could more easily put up with all of it; but search as he might, he couldn't find that *something* inside that the local boys had in excess, so as soon as he started singing, he really did feel like someone who had fallen into the story from some other world and some other time.

'If you're not from this, then what time are you from, stranger?'

'From a past, definitely from a past time that's over, Azra.'

Beautiful Azra's smile was the prize for his effort. She didn't bestow it easily, she hid it a long time, locked away, safely concealed beneath her stern look, which was a reliable jailer.

When they had brought the last boxful of stories downstairs, he sat down on a step and reached into his pocket for a cigarette expecting the conversation to continue. She didn't sit down. She brushed the dust from her slacks and sleeves and quickly went by him up the stairs, as if in some kind of hurry because of carrying all the stories. At the top, she looked back at him.

'Come on, stranger, and you'll see something.'

With a deep breath that didn't express excitement, he got up, cigarette in the corner of his mouth, and slowly, with heavy steps, set off after her. He followed her through the library's first floor, which he knew quite well, asking himself what new thing she could show him there. He looked back several times at the crazy director and the rest of Azra's group, but they were nowhere to be seen. As if they had just up and disappeared. They crossed almost the entire length of the first floor, then she turned left after the last bookshelf. In this part, what was left of the roof still covered them. He thought he knew all the corners of the library well, so the door in the corner behind the last shelf surprised him. How could he have missed it during his visits? It was as if it popped up, appeared out of nowhere. Azra took a key out of her back jeans pocket. She had to lean on the door with her full weight and lift the latch a little for the key to grab and unlock the door. It was dark in the space beyond the door, so he couldn't determine how large it was. She looked around and again invited him with a move of the head to follow.

'Careful of the steps!' she warned him.

After several steps through the dark space, which was clearly some kind of fairly narrow corridor, because despite the total darkness they were slowly wading through, he felt the closeness of a wall, and felt out the first step with his foot. The stairway went down and by the number of steps it seemed quite a bit longer than the one they covered many times in the past hour carrying the books. It was clear they were descending much deeper than the ground floor, maybe into some basement or bunker. He was quiet going down the stairs. He didn't want to ask Azra anything, even though he was filled with curiosity. For an instant he thought of the Kalashnikov he had left leaning in one of the corners. Was he careless? Had he allowed himself to be blinded by a smile that was actually a siren's song, and was he now walking into a trap? He instinctively started to feel for Azra's elbow in the dark, but she was evidently just far enough ahead of him that he couldn't manage to grab it. That alarmed him even more, and he again felt his body filling with jets of adrenaline. He walked a little faster to catch up but he ran into her in two steps. The stairway had apparently ended. That brief second of accidental embrace before he stepped back and said, 'Oops, pardon me, I can't see a thing,' was enough to dispel the awakening fear. As if he was able to see straight into her soul because of the brief contact and was convinced that she had no bad intent. Again he heard the rustling of a key, meaning that they had come to another door at the bottom of the stairs. Azra was opening it slowly, and a strong neon light, which brutally shot from the space beyond and split the total darkness in the corridor, blinded him all the same. He protected his eyes with a palm and turned away a little, then slowly looked back to the illuminated space. Azra was already through the door, she had something substantially different on, but he couldn't determine what. Despite it all, it was doubtless still her. As if in a dream, when the image of a person dreamt constantly changes, but the dream knows all along that it's the same person. She smiled, extended a palm, and invited him to enter. 'Come in, don't be afraid,' her smile said. He stepped into the light.

# MARY

She now knew that it was one of those nights she would not sleep at all. She could have expected that after his departure, but she wondered at how a twenty-year-old story started torturing her instead of the one that just ended. It was snowing harder outside. She opened the window to exchange the thick cigarette smoke for some cold and the smell of fresh snow; it was silence that penetrated her flat more than those two. The snow quieted the huge city, as if in addition to thickly blanketing the pavements, streets, and parked cars it also covered some sort of virtual speakers that transmit street sounds and never go quiet. The speechless city increased her feeling of loneliness even more, so she soon closed the window and turned the sound all the way up. After countless *Catherine the Great* recordings, she was now working through Lennon, whom she never stopped listening to from those days with Denis until now. He introduced her to Lennon on the bank of the river that runs through the city, under long, thin willow branches that danced gently above them. Slowly, almost ritualistically, after having taken a long time to move the tape back and forth to find the right song, he put his Walkman phones to her ears. The sounds of the saxophone washed over her, it sounded like it was playing the last song at a school dance, to which the sweaty couples, leaning against one another, barely move any longer over the already half empty dance floor covered with plastic cups popping under every heavier and tired steps, and the lyrics, the first verses of which sent shivers down her spine. Her first Lennon song was 'Woman is the Nigger of the World'.

She poured her third glass of whiskey and drank it slowly to the sound of the music, without putting it on the table between sips. She thought about how in fact it was good she didn't have a job at the moment. She could make up for the sleepless night in the morning. She had left her last job as a counsellor in a counselling centre not long ago. She simply no longer could take the amount of lies and bullshit that she received every day from people she was supposed to be helping. They started getting on her nerves: drug addicts who were always just about to start treatment but who were in fact just hitting on you for some change; abused women asking you to withdraw the report you sent to the police the day before, like it was a little exaggerated: actually they themselves had provoked the slaps by mouthing off; kids who smeared themselves with war paint before they started shaving. She didn't believe them anymore; she no longer felt any pity for most of them; she preferred to quit rather than become yet another of the indifferent bureaucrats who do their proficient and routine duty every day without the slightest desire or enthusiasm. She was constantly changing cities and jobs since the night in the small Austrian town when she decided to be done with missionary work, changed into jeans and trainers she secretly bought so no one would guess her plans, and walked off to the train station, where she got a one-way ticket to Vienna. She never really stopped from that moment on. They were all just longer or shorter stops on the road that wound from uncontrolled thirsting for freedom, via aimless rambling and searching, to yet another destination. A destination that always turned out to be mistaken, or simply a way-station to the next one.

**Recording 3**

An Amsterdam club with live music. Saturday evening and the bar is packed solid. Now she's moving easily through the crowd with a full tray of drinks held high above her head, her right arm almost fully extended, while her left gently moves people in the way aside. Having clumsily broken glasses and bottles and being unable to find her way through the thicket of bodies, in one month, she turned into an agile, ubiquitous waitress who quickly moved through the crowd without stopping, like an illusionist through a wall. She's already used to her body capturing looks as it sways through the crowd of guests like a cobra at a fakir's pipe. She knows how effortlessly to escape conversations that start with bows and generally continue with the man's monologue about himself.

'Me and my friend have been talking about you for almost half an hour.'

On account of the loud music (Cobain's version of Bowie's 'The Man Who Sold the World' is an excellent musical background for her current stage of life), the somewhat darker skinned young fellow who had stopped her with his arm comes very close to her ear. He speaks English with a Balkan accent. The number of students from the Balkans at the close-by university increased proportionately to the spread of the war, so she knew the accent well.

'Yeah? What about me?'

She chews her gum without smiling and looks him right in the eye, as if checking whether he would dare be a further nuisance.

'We'd like to know which one of us will take you home tonight. We are savages from Balkans, you know, where the war is.'

The metros in pastel shirts and sweaters passing themselves off as exotic wild men are gradually getting on her nerves with their perverse desire to make a small profit from the war they ran from, as far as their legs and parents' financial wherewithal could take them.

'So why aren't you down there killing each other if you're such savages? Your daddies paid your way out or what?'

Her reply is quick because it was prepared. Her reply takes all the wind out of the sails of the dark-haired one in a Lacoste t-shirt and the blonde in a green Benetton jacket. They look at each other and for lack of a good answer howl ridiculously. Now that the two are completely on the defensive, she leans towards the dark-haired one.

'You can wait for me at two in front of the club, but don't talk to me until then, OK?'

She continues on to the bar and doesn't give them even one more look until the end of the evening. At four in the morning, when she had made her way from the bedroom to the door and put on her things, she's already leaving their shared flat. It was a solid fuck. The dark-haired one, partly due to the alcohol and partly to her insistence on taking control the moment they entered the flat, held it long enough for her to climax in his arms, for which he earned only an indulgent peck on the right cheek instead of the kiss he expected.

New York, along with the one who just left her, the flat and job at the counselling centre was clearly not what she was successfully sold on for several years. After the next glass, which followed the one that was one too many, she already knew that one of the coming days her life would once again be in a suitcase, and she on a plane, train, or silver Greyhound bus. She would be on the road again.

'Fuckin' Google doesn't know everything after all.'

She turned off and closed the laptop when she couldn't find any, not the smallest trace of Denis in it. Denis's total absence was almost unbelievable from the perspective of the era of digital cameras and smartphones, when every fleeting and usual moment is recorded in at least five photos and immediately shared on social media. Is it possible Denis is even alive if he leaves no traces on the internet? Did he ever really live? Not long ago, on a natural rink on a frozen lake at the edge of the city, she was watching a large group of young people getting ready for a curling match. The young men really worked hard to prepare all that was needed: they smoothed a long, square patch of ice, drew two large targets at both ends with red spray paint, brought enough brooms and stones with handles affixed for hurling that were clearly home-made. And instead of starting the match, hurling the large granite stones over the smooth path and helping them slide to the target by sweeping, they took pictures of one another pretending to hurl, pretending to sweep, pretending to celebrate a point, pretending to live. The curling match that Mary waited for with interest as she skated circles on the other side didn't even ever take place on the frozen lake in the suburbs: it would take place only later, in the imaginations of the group's friends and acquaintances when they viewed the countless pictures on the internet. Do the pictures and recordings we preserve exclusively in the files of our memories lie to us in the same way? Did things really happen the way we remember them?

### Recording 4

Denis, Peter and Goran laugh out loud, at first genuinely, then, as they go on, it's more and more forced, like teenagers who want to show as many passers-by as possible what a good time they're having. Peter and Goran walk ahead, handing off a bottle of wine, which they also offer Denis. She doesn't drink at all, and Denis declines a swig as well, probably because of her. They had already emptied one in the park, before evening fell, and Peter and Goran will clearly finish the second on the way to the concert hall. They've been walking the main street about a half hour, they just passed the stadium, and now they're happily and loudly marching along a long green fence surrounding a building with large windows. Most of them are open, only at one are there two shadows seated, between which a small bright light moves. Just when Denis is about to ask what's in the building, whether it's a hospital or something like that, a soldier comes up to them on the other side of the fence. The olive green helmet with a red star in the middle is a little too big for him, so was cocked somewhat down on the right side of his face. He walks clumsily, like a bear. Apparently expecting a cold evening and night, he had put a sweater on under his overcoat that was secured with a wide leather belt and shoulder straps. The moment they pass by him, Denis, Peter and Goran quiet down a little and don't even direct a quick look at him. The soldier only turns his eyes towards them, without so much as tilting his head in their direction. He's young, just a year or so older than them probably. The soldier took a few more steps on his way from the point they passed each other, then turned around and started to follow them. He walked a little faster than them, so he was now slowly and surely catching up. Mary was uncomfortable: she felt the five-pointed red star on his helmet was a threat. She pulls Denis's shoulder and whispers in his ear:

'The soldier, Denis. He's following us.'

Denis is surprised she's worried, instinctively looks around, and sees that the solder is indeed following them.

'Don't worry, they're like watchdogs, always behind the fence'.

When they get to the corner, where the old Austro-Hungarian iron fence surrounding the military building the soldier was guarding turns left, their path goes straight across the street. They hear a hushed call in Serbo-Croatian from behind them.

'Heah, pssst, heah guys, you got a smoke? Some dope? No, no, don't turn around! Stand still and just nod if you have something to smoke.'

Mary, not understanding a word, grips Denis' hand tighter, while he slowly and tentatively exchanges looks with Peter and Goran.

'Screw it, let's give him a joint, fuck it, in two years we're going to be like that, asking the locals for something in some poor, god-forsaken village.'

'What's he saying, Denis? What's he want from us?'

'Oh, nothing, Mary, he's just asking if we can spare a cigarette. Give him one, Goran, and let's go.'

Goran is just at the point of spasmodic laughter; giggling idiotically, he starts approaching the fence and the soldier behind it backwards. He's holding a joint behind his back, and pushes it through the wire. When he feels the soldier grab it, he lets go. He doesn't stop giggling through the whole transaction.

'Scuse me, guys, you saved my life. It's nuts, there's no leave, because of that shit with Janša and those stolen documents. You? You going to dinner?'

The soldier wants to keep up contact with the outside world a little longer.

'To a concert. The Croatian band, Azra.'

'My God Azra? Azra you say? Wish I could go.'

Mary doesn't understand a word of the conversation and doesn't know what Goran means when he says, 'Heh, man, want me to sub for you?' So his leap over the fence, which ends practically in the soldier's arms, surprises her even more.

'Give me that helmet, overcoat, and rifle, I'll do your guard duty, and you go to the concert, put on my jacket...'

While Goran, still giggling like an idiot, and the soldier change clothes, Denis, Peter and Mary nervously keep watch, each in a different direction. Denis explains to her what is going on. He says it's OK, because before long the three of them will be in the soldier's shoes.

'You know, just like in *Hair*, when the boss hippie takes that soldier's place. Only in this case, Goran for sure won't end up in Vietnam.'

'Yeah, but he could end up in Kosovo,' says Peter.

'Peter is saying he might end up in Kosovo,' Denis explains to Mary in English, 'that is... ahhh, forget it.You wouldn't understand about Kosovo anyway.'

The concert is wild. During 'The Balkans', Azra's frontman jumps into the crowd and whacks two drunk fans who bloodied his upper lip by banging on the stage so hard they knocked over the microphone. The escaped soldier finds a girl for the night who even accompanies him to the barracks after the concert and to boot promises to return on Sunday and request they let him out for an hour or two. Goran is waiting for them where they left him. He isn't going to Kosovo, but he's pretty frozen.

The new pack of cigarettes was running out, and there were several more hours to morning. When she pushed the building door open and stepped into the street, it was like stepping into some Impressionist painting; the title could have been 'A Snow Storm in New York'. It was snowing so heavily that all the straight lines and edges were invisible. Only vaguely. Discernible outlines were all that remained of the city, its skyscrapers, streets, and street numbers behind the thick curtain of snow. If she looked up, large snowflakes fell right in her eyes and melted like icy tears on her cheeks. She walked down the middle of the street a snowplough had just cleared. The parked cars on both sides were slowly changing into large snow sculptures of different sizes. It seemed like she was all alone in the street. Given the hour and the weather conditions, she didn't expect to meet anyone. She started and froze for a few seconds when twenty metres ahead a tall male figure in a long, dark coat slid into the street from behind one of the snowed-in cars. Because of his unsuitable shoes – he had on what looked pretty much like summer dress shoes – he was hopelessly slipping and it looked like he would land on his back at any moment. He didn't have a hat on, so his wet pate shone like a lightbulb as he gripped a pile of books in his arms. She didn't know whether he noticed her, but in any case, he didn't pay attention to her. He went down the street as if in a hurry with quick, sliding steps. Unlike Mary, the pedestrian in the dark coat obviously knew very well where he was headed. Mary, who until now had been aimlessly strolling the deserted streets, started walking after him without even being aware of it. She was curious where the person with a pile of books in his arms could have been going at that hour in such weather. She gave no thought to what she was doing as long as he went ahead along the main, illuminated street; she only increased the distance between them a little so that he wouldn't notice. But when after a good five minutes he turned into a dark side street, she hesitated. Perhaps he had noticed her and was trying to lure her into a trap, or he was running from her and just trying to hide? She was somewhat frightened at the first possibility and became embarrassed at the second thought. It was certainly not clever to follow a stranger in the big city at night for no reason, yet she continued towards the small, dark street. First she just took a peek around the corner. It was hard to see, the street was dark, only way down at the end a small light illuminated a cellar stairway her quarry's pate was descending at that moment, which calmed her somewhat. At least now she knew he wasn't lying in wait for her in some unlit, dark corner between her and the stairway, which looked like the entrance to some nightclub. From where she was standing, there was no lettering or sign visible by the stairway that might have satisfied her curiosity, which was too great for a few dozen metres of an unlit street to quell. She briefly pressed her eyes closed, took two deep breaths, then held her breath as if preparing to go under water, and ran through the dark corridor towards the illuminated stairway. Of course, no snowplough had passed there, so she cleared a path through the calf-deep snow in the dark, but the snow was so light that it seemed to part before her steps even before she really touched it.

She quickly left behind the several dozen metres of darkness. She stood at the top of the stairway and looked down at the door. To the right was a sign she was unable to read because of the poor light and distance from the top of the stairs. She slowly started down and about halfway she could read the words on the simple plaque: BALKANICA LIBRARY. She halted. Was such an absurd conclusion to the evening really possible?

'It's like I'm in some Paul Auster novel.'

Least of all did she expect to actually find what the sign promised – an apparently 24/7 Balkan library – behind the door. Yet the windowless wooden door gave her no response. There was no bell, so she would simply have to walk in. Should she knock first? While she carefully stretched a hand to the door, the copperplate latch jerked away, the door opened, and the space it had fit in between the jambs was filled by the figure dressed in a black coat she followed along the snowy streets. He went by her without hesitation, as if through her, with quick steps. She had to squeeze right up against the wall so he didn't knock her to the ground as he went. Nothing in his expression or in his eyes indicated he noticed her at all. Pressed to the wall, she watched him until he disappeared over the horizon at the top of the stairs. Then she again turned towards the door. It remained open. It didn't open onto some small cellar space that a person might expect, given the location and entrance sign promising a boutique library dedicated to a limited geographical area. The extent of the space behind the door was not visible. It seemed to be bordered by only the ceiling and floor, she couldn't see walls on the sides. It was doubtless a library, because countless bookshelves were arrayed in the space, and books of various formats, colours, and thicknesses crowded them, without having the appearance of being arranged in any kind of order. Thrown together in this way, they rather gave the impression of some logically observed disorder. Quite a few people were strolling between the shelves, not communicating with each other with words or looks. It was as if each of them was completely alone in this huge space. Only Mary, now holding her soaked coat in her arms, curiously looked over the space and people, who showed no interest in her. They were of all ages, dressed appropriately for different times of the year. A lot of them wore light coloured work-out clothes, while some of them were in winter coats. An old lady with a fox-fur around her neck attracted her attention. Both of them were totally focused on the bookshelves and blissfully ignorant of the other visitors. She walked between the bookshelves, along some main street with outlets left and right into numerous smaller streets, the ends of which couldn't be seen from where she was standing; they grew continually narrower between the very closely arranged shelves. After several steps, when she was somewhat accustomed to no one noticing her, she saw a woman maybe a dozen metres ahead acting as the centre of this limitless space. As if all the countless bookshelves were placed around her and all the people not looking at one another were gravitating towards her according to some inner law of the space. She's a librarian, has to be a librarian. Unlike all the others in the hall, she looked directly at Mary, even beamed at her, like a hostess whose long-awaited guest had arrived. When she approached her, Mary's eyes rested on her remarkably long white neck adorned by a thin, gold chain, and her dark eyes that beamed even more than her face.

'Welcome, Mary, we've been expecting you.'

# PETER & GORAN

At first everything was as usual when Peter woke up in the morning. Nothing special. But it remained that way for only a few minutes, then – not slowly, in individual drops, but all at once, in a powerful gush – the entire story of the past night in all its bizarreness flowed into his head, in which pain was slowly welling up. At first, of course, he thought that it was a dream, but he recalled the conversation with Goran and the feelings that overwhelmed him vividly and with crystal clarity, as he never did with dreams. He reached to the edge of the marital bed – that was now too wide – in one roll and leapt from it much more quickly than when taking a few moments to stretch and do the scratching necessary on the itchy parts of his back, arms, and rear. With decisive, quick steps emphasized by powerful footfalls on the cold parquet, at which he recalled in passing that he really had to put down some kind of rug to replace the one Tanja liked so much she had to take it away, he marched to the living room to check the roster of calls. If Goran's call was recorded, then he in fact took it, and if not, it didn't happen and 'So I just dreamed it' he decided. For weeks now, an image awaited him in the anteroom mirror that had a worse hair condition than the one he had projected the day before. True, there were also those several exceptional mornings when a somewhat overweight, middle-aged man in the mirror was not wearing wrinkled pants and a t-shirt from the day before, but was at least in his underwear if not pyjamas. This wasn't an exceptional morning. He was still in yesterday's pants and shirt. Good thing he had managed to toss aside the windbreaker the night before, which unlike his trousers, completely wrinkled and pulled a quarter turn around his rear, he could put on again today. Outside it was a dark and miserable morning, it hadn't yet started to rain, but Peter knew the worst morning downpour would come exactly at the moment he would have to take those several steps in the parking lot from the building to his car. He remembered that after the supposed conversation with Goran and before tackling the remaining cans of beer he had in the refrigerator, he put his phone on the upper bookshelf. That was precisely where he found it, which again confused him a little. After being awake several minutes, he was almost sure that last night's conversation with his friend, locked in his own suitcase, had taken place only in his dreams, and that he would find proof of that in the living room. He directly began pressing the buttons until he came to the call list, in which there was no trace of Goran's night-time call. 'OK., damn good' he let out a breath at the conclusion that despite everything the improbable stories still remained in the dream realm. He put the phone back in the same place, turned on the radio in the kitchen, and put water on for coffee, which he planned on drinking while listening to the early morning news and having his first cigarette, which he had already lit.

He waited as the water dithered shamefully and refused to boil, ready with a spoon in one hand and plastic container in the other to stir the fragrant roasted grind into the bubbles. In the meantime, the rhythm of an old Stones number burst forth into his neglected kitchen from the crackling speakers of the radio he kept on the kitchen counter exclusively for this morning plugging into the world: 'We all need someone we can dream on ♪ and if you want it, you can dream on me ♪.' The rock 'n roll hit filled the space and his rounded body started imperceptibly to sway at the hips, slowly back and forth, and his right hand, holding the spoon, started strumming an air guitar hanging low under his hip, like it always hangs on Keith. He started mimicking him by allowing his cigarette to carelessly drop to the edge of his mouth. His left hand, on the neck of his air guitar, tried to catch the movements, his fingers forming C, F, G, and E chords as he got more into the unexpected morning performance before his espresso cup, and pile of unwashed dishes.

His acoustic Fender, which he hadn't taken up for more than ten years, as a stubborn layer of almost eternal dust on the black case in which it had been carefully placed and locked attested, was propped in the corner of a dusty shed fifteen floors below, filled with cast-off parts of a child's bed, ski equipment, New Year's decorations, and a plastic tree. But it wasn't utterly lonely in the packed basement. The top of the neck of Denis's bass stuck out of a large box filled with old books from his student years. Later that day, that day Peter and Goran had spoken about, Peter brought it from practice and kept it under his bed for a long time, convinced that one of the following days Denis would show up at his door. When that expectation quickly dimmed with the passing weeks, disappeared with the months and years, and his parents moved out to the cottage to make room for the young family, he first took the bass and later his guitar and put them away in the shed. As the years went by, he turned it into a kind of time capsule for keeping once important things that with time get in a person's way.

His morning kitchen performance didn't last long, since he had turned on the radio when the song was almost half over, and the water boiled at exactly the moment he was most caught up in the air solo and took his eye off it. 'Ah, fuck!' he cursed when it frothed over the edge of the coffee pot and spilled over the range.

In the morning he always treated himself to real Turkish coffee together with the whole ritual of preparing it, the copper *cezve* and small espresso cup that drove Tanja nuts in recent years.

Her Nescafe was always ready in a few minutes, while his morning coffee ripened at least about five. The trick was to pour off half the water in the *cezve* just before it boiled so that he could sprinkle a small amount of coffee into the remaining half, which he then boiled three times, pouring in the saved water at the end. And the moment, the instant when the water was about to boil, he would often, this morning as well, divert his attention. Of course, he didn't know of a rational explanation for why it was so important to catch that instant, brief as a wink, but all the same he always tried to keep to the prescribed procedure. The fact that his morning ritual drove Tanja with her large cup of Nescafe nuts as she ran around the flat dressing the little one and herself only made it more fun for him.

After the Stones came a news story that didn't appeal to him in the least, and he calmly continued preparing his coffee. He saw that all his small espresso cups were grimy with the condensed remains of yesterday's, the day-before-yesterday's, and morning coffees from the past three or four days, so he set about washing them. It wasn't so simple without a sponge, and he only got most of the brown marks off the white porcelain by constant rubbing with a finger. Only a thin brown circle remained on the bottom, and he decided to ignore it. The introduction to the next story on the radio news caught his ear at that moment, and though he kept up his routine, mechanically preparing the coffee, his attention was totally directed at the news broadcaster's voice as she faultlessly and objectively reported about what she termed 'an unusual event'.

'Late yesterday afternoon, a building of a small industrial firm was occupied by employees who apparently lost patience after not having received their regular pay for more than four months. They are holding the director and several members of his staff in the management offices. Strikers are guarding the entrance to the place and not allowing anyone to enter or leave. The police decided against intervening so as not to threaten the safety of the company's management who are being held hostage. They are instead negotiating with the workers, who give assurances that neither the director nor anyone in management is for now in danger, but that they will insist on their demands until they are met. According to unofficial sources, they are demanding a transfer of unpaid wages from foreign accounts to which management is said to have redirected the company's receipts. Our team is also going to the site and will send us reports on events as they evolve.'

He appeared calmly to boil the contents of the *cezve* a third time, put it aside, put a sugar cube in a small cup, pour the coffee over it, light another cigarette, and sit down at the table. He always sat on the very edge of the chair, as if wanting to give the impression that he was actually already on his way, that any minute he would get up and go to the bathroom. Despite this, he always sat at the table almost motionless for some long, quiet minutes, during which his left wrist made small, even circles with the cup and with his right hand he smoked his second morning cigarette.

He got used to drinking his morning coffee alone long before Tanja finally left. The entire year before she didn't sit down with him, with the exception of the morning she informed him of her intention to leave. She had no use for any talk even then, she only desired to acquaint him with the decision she had made with as little spectacle as possible; he had suspected it for some time.

'Peter, I can't go on. Luka and I are leaving. I found a flat nearby. This weekend Luka will be at my mum's so I can pack up our things, and I'm counting on us sleeping in the new flat on Sunday.'

Despite having anticipated her decision, he didn't have an answer prepared, and so he simply looked through her for several minutes, saying nothing, and swirling his coffee cup. Since she had said all she intended, she just sat there waiting in vain for any sort of reaction. Silence didn't bother him, he felt at home in it, for it was his old hideaway, to which he always retreated in the face of her criticisms and accusations. In contrast, the lack of an answer drove her nuts.

'What's with you? You got nothing to say? Say something, anything, so I know you at least heard me, you fuck!'

As always when she managed to flush him from his silent refuge, and he was pressured to say something, he only made matters worse.

'You got somebody else or what?'

Although she received the oldest, most expected, and worn male reply, she was surprised at him. She looked at him with a mix of pity and hate, apparently deciding whether to say anything more or simply get up from the table and leave. In the end she just grabbed his hand to stop him from swirling the cup, shook her head a few times, and smiled barely perceptibly. Then she left.

Now he was again convinced that the past night he had talked with Goran, who was probably still hiding in his suitcase from the crazed workers. He again reached for his phone, looked for Goran's number, and called. 'The person is currently not available. Please call later.'

He left the ashtray with two butts and the cup with thick coffee grounds stuck to the bottom on the kitchen table with a plastic cover decorated with some brown traces, the coffee marks of several mornings. Clouds of cigarette smoke still danced against the ceiling around the large orange sideboard that Peter's mum had bought at the end of the 1970s. The stench of the two butts in the ashtray soon started to overcome the pleasant smell when big, fat drops started hitting the window, breaking into long rivulets that slowly crawled down the glass. The drops rushed out of the dark morning without slowing, as if trying to catch Peter, who was riding the lift down to the building door.

Every time he ran to his car in a downpour, he thought about where he last left his umbrella, tried to avoid puddles, and in advance greeted that warm moment when he would shove himself behind the wheel, soaked. He would close the car door behind him and the sound of rain would instantly change from a quiet, constant noise into the loud drumming of drops on the roof. The stench of the extinguished cigarettes coming from the ashtray under the radio ruined the anticipated idyll of the small, dry space. He had intended to empty it somewhere for a few days but didn't find the right moment. Today, he thought with conviction, today is the day he would certainly empty it, he would get back out of the car and go to the nearest container, where he would quickly dump it, if it only weren't pouring so hard. His ageing blue station wagon would thus have to wait for cleaning at least until the rain let up, until then it would have to put up with several more butts Peter would stuff into the overflowing ashtray. The downpour was so heavy that he saw nothing but water ahead, pouring down the windshield. He fished a pack of Fisherman's Friend from the slot in the armrest. He always sucked on them driving to work after a hellish night like the last one. Despite the strong coffee, his hands were not yet completely calm, they kept shaking, and the candies accidentally fell between his legs and under his rear, which caused him to look down and see that his fly was wide open. 'Oh, damn!' What a poor impression, of a pathetic, old drunk he must have made on the new, young neighbour who joined him on the ninth floor and rode all the way down to the basement in silence, staring on the floors flying by, as strangers do in lifts, and then gave him a brief glance and 'good-bye' so as to at least give the appearance of reducing their age difference. He calmly looked at her fresh, round behind elegantly swaying in front of him for several moments. 'Maybe she didn't notice,' he thought. After all, only his dark briefs were visible through the open fly, the whole thing could have been a lot uglier if the edge of his white undershirt found its way out of the inadvertent slit.

A look ahead at the morning swarm of cars, which was larger than usual due to the rain, and then at the dashboard clock left no doubt: if at the intersection he turned towards the closest bypass, in the direction of the occupied factory, instead of towards downtown, he would certainly be late for his nine o'clock meeting at the ministry. When he would finally appear with all the traces of the past night, which couldn't be fully washed from his face, the talk of how he had completely lost control of his drinking would get even worse. Not that he had any intention of participating much in the meeting. Did he have anything sensible to say about a law that mandates the use of Slovene and prescribes fines for violations. About an idea that could only well up in some forgotten, dark intestine of the state administration's obscure belly, where hidden from view and voices of reason it grows to a critical mass, at which point it cannot be painlessly and safely removed. He could only once again, perhaps a tad more colourfully than before, express his conviction that it would be like to legislate the act of breathing. There would be not a few, at first red-faced and then completely blue, who would hold their breath convinced that their freedom depended on a lack of air. After hesitating a few seconds, he finally decided and yanked the wheel sharply to the left. He removed his station wagon from the long column that would slowly, from traffic light to traffic light, make its way downtown, to the neighbouring, entirely empty lane and easily slipped by the standing cars to the intersection, where he turned left.

A scene worthy of some action film awaited him at Stepinšek's company: police, ambulance, and fire vehicles with quietly rotating blue lights crowded in front of the main entrance to the factory forecourt, which was closed off behind a large green gate, secured with a thick chain. The rain was wiping the black spray-painted letters O C C U P A T I O N!, exclamation point, off the sheet over the gate. Peter smirked at the letter C, forcefully shoved as an afterthought between C and U. He imagined a worker setting to work on the banner in the middle of all the confusion and uproar: how he carefully, slowly, in a hand not used to graffiti first sprayed O, then C, making very sure the letters and spaces between them were about the same size, and how, having just finished the U, he noticed he forgot a C... 'Ahhh,' thought Peter, he must have uttered a juicy curse, perhaps even smacked a palm on his forehead before he started to fix it.

A pretty large crowd made up almost entirely of women standing on their tiptoes and trying to catch but a fleeting glimpse of their husbands, calmly stood on the grass the rain had turned into a large, muddy swamp on the other side of the blockade made up of vehicles with blue lights, between which special units in full gear had taken up positions. Some brought their children, squeezing under umbrellas with them. The little ones lay in their arms and watched all the colourful vehicles and uniformed men with big eyes; the older ones squirmed at their sides, bored, looking up and trying to read from their mothers' faces what was going on. Worry and pride fought for space on their faces, with the latter markedly surging to the fore as a comforting reward for all the previous days and months of shame and then despair at their want. When Peter slowly and respectfully pushed ahead through the crowd and was again soaked by the rain, he noticed packed duffel bags hanging from the women's shoulders. Jasmina from the North Side stood alone, almost at the very front, without children but with a fully packed Puma duffel. She didn't notice him until he tugged on her elbow.

'Heh, Jasmina, what's goin' on? Is Milan inside or what?'

She was his age, she lived some buildings down from him, was basically very pretty, but always in the company of older boys. She soon married Milan, who was a few years older, right out of school, their two children of course had to be in secondary school already. She was surprised to see him there.

'Yeah, he's inside. Since yesterday. He called me on his mobile. That they occupied the factory, and that… until they get their pay, for me to bring some clothes and food, 'cause they don't know how long it'll go on. Only when I got here, there were already police, and they're not letting people in. Some women got to throw their bags over the fence before they parked the trucks. So why are you here?'

'Well, it's a long story really. And a strange one. This morning I heard on the radio, and at night I got a… strange call from Goran. You know, Goran? He works here in sales or something. I got a little worried about him.'

'Ahh', her voice trailed off and instantly cooled, 'you're worried about that little pussy? I'm as bothered by the fix he's in as he was about us when he didn't have… damn, we didn't have anything to eat, Pero!'

They were now starting to attract other women's looks, Jasmina's voice began to crack, she was at the point of succumbing to tears, so he tried talking as quietly as possible, hoping she would follow his lead. After he quietly said, 'I know, I know', several times, and Jasmina forced herself to calm down, he nonetheless tried to find out from her what was happening inside.

'Can you still call Milan now?'

'Yeah, I can.'

'Please ask him how Goran is, if he's even inside or not.'

'I'm not gonna call him for that filth, you got me? It's obvious he is, I can see his fag convertible over there, parked by the factory.'

'Where?'

'Over there, the white one, next to Stepinšek's BMW,' she pointed inside the forecourt, where they could see through the iron gate's bars, under the sheet with the sign that was hanging more and more sadly on account of the rain.

So, it was clear Goran was inside, which further confirmed their night-time conversation was real.

'Look, Jasmina, this is no joke, your Milan and the rest of the workers inside obviously decided to take matters into their own hands, and now there are some kind of new, maybe really more just laws over the fence. Only once they come out, everything will be waiting for them the way it was, the police and all ...'

She started looking at him differently. No longer as a neighbour and kid from the North Side with whom you share common haunts, memories, and acquaintances, but as one of Them; those who were guilty for her troubles. In less than a minute a canyon opened between them, and it only grew wider, so he tried to extend a hand rather than threaten.

'I get it that they lost it if he was really robbing them like that, and that's why it seems to me wrong that in the end they'll be even more fucked if they don't know where to stop. They'll let them off for a few pranks, if nothing worse happens, and I'll put in a good word for them at the ministry.'

He didn't say at which ministry he worked, so he actually didn't lie to her, but he said the word 'ministry' in such a way that she surely had the impression he worked in internal affairs, where his good word could really have meant something. He wasn't proud of his little manipulation, quite the contrary, but at the moment it was more important for him to get some information about Goran. Although he had the impression that the hate in her eyes was only growing and that he had inflamed it by trying to convince her, she slowly reached into a pocket and pulled out her phone. She didn't give Peter another look as she waited for an answer from the other side of the barricade; he stood behind her, and she stared through the fence; he didn't know any more than before whether she had any intention of meeting his request.

'Milan, how are you? Aha, yeah… if they transferred it yet? I don't know, I can check, I have to go to the bank or maybe a cash machine. Are you all right? Heh, there's this Peter here… you know, from the North Side? He wants to ask you something. Well, about that Goran in there.'

Without turning around, she stuck out her hand with the phone.
    'Heh, Milan… Goran called me last night from his office…'

Of course, he didn't intend to tell Milan the story of Goran getting locked in his suitcase, because Milan would most probably tell him where to go, and he wouldn't learn anything. On the other hand, he didn't sense any of the inspiration that should have, in his opinion, gone with any revolution and its revolutionaries, no matter how minor. Only worry and weariness. He recognized the silence in the background. It was the same foreboding silence that framed last night's conversation with Goran.

'Really? He was in his office? We didn't see him. His office was empty when we went there, he was nowhere around, so it seems he took off when we were in Stepinšek's.'

'What about his suitcase? Is it still in the office? Go on and take a look, please…'

He heard Milan walking and then stop, open the door, and go in. Then he put the phone to his ear again.

'Yeah, it's here. The suitcase is here.'

'Can you open it and take a look what's inside?'

Peter was surprised at his own anxiety as on the other end he first heard the phone put down on the desk and then the clicking of the small latches on Goran's Samsonite. As if he admitted the possibility of Milan actually finding his lost friend in the suitcase.

'There's just his fancy phone inside. Turned off.'

'OK Milan, thanks. Hang in there, and don't do anything stupid with the director.'

'Yeah, no worries. Don't panic, looks like we're going to let him go soon anyway, 'cause he supposedly already ordered the money into our accounts. The boys are checking.'

Peter returned the phone to Jasmina, who continued her conversation with Milan, still standing on tiptoe, her feet sinking even deeper into the soft, muddy muck, her eyes on the barricade. He headed back to his car through the throng. Goran wouldn't even go to bed without his Blackberry, and if he somehow managed to disappear from the office, he surely would have taken his smartphone with him. He was once again at the beginning of his questions about last night's events.

When he finally broke through the forest of women's bodies and umbrellas, which offered him a temporary refuge, the rain again started incessantly drenching him. Behind his back he heard at first a quiet two, three voices, then a louder, but all the more determined, if disjointed, song arise. 'Arise ye workers from your slumbers,' and so on all the way to the end, when the soaked women with duffel bags on their shoulders and umbrellas in their hands really gave it their all and screamed at the top of their voices for the people to unite and rush to the final battle. He turned around for a second and took a look at the forest of different coloured umbrellas swaying in front of the barricade from beneath which echoed a song of times past, times of May Day celebrations and red kerchiefs. This time as in the past, when at various events people took up this or some other worn revolutionary or partisan song, the whole thing seemed to him hopelessly pathetic; it didn't spark anything in him but acerbic cynicism.

He recalled the recent celebration of his mum's sixtieth birthday, when towards the end of the party, when most of the guests were slouched spent in their chairs only waiting for the Styrian sour soup, Uncle Stane took a guitar from one of the band members and started wailing *Hasta siempre, Comandante,* and forged on quietly to the approval of those of mum's contemporaries who were present, expressed only in the nods of tired heads, which at the peak of the refrain turned into group calls to the *comandante* and shaking of clenched fists. If Peter had by some miracle been sober or at least not too high, as most of the others were, he would have allowed it to pass. But since he had been silently imbibing red wine the whole evening while hardly eating, an incident was practically unavoidable. He waited until Stane finished singing the concluding call to the *comandante,* earning a short applause, took another puff, and then said sarcastically, 'What do you think, Uncle Stane, what'll the scene be like when you and your *compañeros* drive to the next revolution in your Mercedes, BMWs, and Porsches? Folks will see for themselves what motherfuckers you are.'

Uncle Stane, who had left his job at the Ministry of Internal Affairs a few years earlier and become a director in one of the large state enterprises, where things were going well indeed, as was evidenced in his expanding car lot, ended the unpleasant silence, during which Peter caught his mum's pleading look, with a pretty poorly affected laugh, followed by an attempt to humiliate and silence Peter.

'Pete, you've had a little too much again? Come on, don't ruin your mum's celebration, be nice.'

'Yeah, yeah, Uncle Stane, I'll be NICE and quiet, 'cause that suits you and your kind, when we're nice and quiet and polite, so you can erase and rip people off in peace, right?'

He said the last part on his way to the door, towards which his sobbing mum was pulling him. When he looked back at Uncle Stane, he saw him shaking his head in disappointment.

When he thought it over, he decided for himself it wasn't the same story, and he couldn't allow himself to be cynical about those women in the rain, their feet in the mud, singing at the barricade, so before getting back in the car, far behind their backs, he raised a fist in the air and sang the last refrain with them; contrary to his cynicism (of which he was full), he admitted to himself that he felt pretty good.

On the way back, even before the rain had completely stopped, the sun started to break through the clouds, which had a tight grip on the city in the morning and were now slowly but surely letting go. The last raindrops, together with the first rays of sun, created a blinding glint on his windshield, turning the road, cars, trees, and houses by the side into dark shadows. He squinted hard to make out at least something of what was going on right in front of his car. On the part of the route where the road leaves the neighbourhoods and follows long, gentle turns through a wood, he was surprised by a shelter right in the middle of the trees, like some bus stop, from under which a dark silhouette was rising, a hand extended towards the road. He never stopped for hitch-hikers, so he decided to leave this one behind, too. When he came even with the stop without any sign of braking, and the silhouette moved back from the road a step, the shadow was lifted from her face. It was a woman younger than him. She looked after his car, and after driving by, he, too, didn't stop looking at her. It seemed to him that she was smiling as if she knew him, as if it was him she was waiting for in the middle of the woods. The blue station wagon first slowed and then, when its bright red brake lights came on, stopped still several dozen metres from the hitch-hiker standing under the shelter at the bus stop over which tall firs rose, surely too tall for this area. She kept looking at him. Her hands were hidden deep in the pockets of a dark, tightly belted raincoat that emphasized her slender body, and its wide collar raised high hid most of her face. He saw in the rear-view mirror how she continued to stare at his car, as if it was her only chance, as if no other would come down the road after it. Thinking this, he couldn't overlook the fact that the road had become unusually deserted since he drove into the wooded section, though he hadn't paid any attention to it until now. When the white back-up lights came on in place of the red brake lights, Peter's station wagon started slowly reversing towards the stranger, who kept standing motionless in the same place. He came up beside her with the passenger-side window already down, and the smiling face of a brown-haired girl with large dark eyes peered into the smoky interior.

'I was afraid you wouldn't stop.'

The way she started talking, as if they knew each other or were at least the same age, pleased him, although he was surprised. After checking out of the corner of his eye whether his fly was right now, he leaned over to open the passenger door, trying his best to return the woman's friendly, mildly flirtatious smile.

'You going to town?'

She didn't answer his question, but just got in, ran a hand through her soaked, quite short hair. Peter thought that Someone was obviously having some good fun with him: people disappearing into suitcases, workers occupying a factory, and now a soaked, sexy hitch-hiker in a raincoat appears to him in the middle of a wood.

'You miss the bus?'

'Not really.'

'Aha, I get it, so you were trying to hitch-hike while you waited for it'.

'Something like that.'

'So where should I let you off?'

'Just drive, I'll tell you where to stop.'

She wasn't smiling any longer, but she still had a warm, friendly look. Understanding she didn't want to talk, he stopped asking questions and paid a little more attention to his driving. The wood they were driving through became thicker and darker, and there were still no other cars to be seen. He couldn't recall where he might have gone wrong, but he certainly had never driven this way.

'Does this road even go to town?'

Instead of answering, she just shook her head, and despite the fact that his hands were on the wheel, he had a strong sense that it was actually the mysterious young woman next to him who was driving, and not the other way around.

# DENIS, 1990

'Oh, fuck, the little Mormon's got a heavy hand,' it struck him just before he first sat and then lay down on the ground after Brother Noah struck his cheekbone with a hard right. It was the first serious, real cinematic punch he had ever taken. He had suffered some shoves, grabbed collars, kicks of varying force, but never before had a tightly clenched male fist crashed into his face. He felt the full strength of the punch, because it completely shook him, but there was no pain at all, contrary to all his previous notions of how it would be. It was as if the cheekbone the young Mormon's fist approached in a flash, and retreated from just as quickly, was not his own, or as if he had a local anaesthetic in that part of his face just before the fight and so he didn't feel any pain from the punch. From the countless descriptions of fights he had heard the last several years and seen live, he knew that the position he was now in was one of the least favourable you could find yourself in during a fight. He was lying on the ground in front of a high rise on the edge of a central city park where he had come to settle accounts with the male part of the Mormon mission, surrounded by three pairs of black, fairly worn shoes, carefully covered with shoe polish and freshly buffed with a rag. He knew it would be wise to protect his face and crotch with his hands, but he didn't do it fast or effectively enough. Since he wasn't surrounded by three skinheads or some Bosnians versed in fighting techniques, he didn't really expect a kick to follow Noah's direct right. He got it in the forehead, with which Denis had started the fight in the first place, right in the painful area sporting an impression of Brother Kenyon's lower front teeth.

Denis had gone into the courtyard of the old building where the young Mormon missionaries lived just a few minutes before the moment that found Brother Noah, Brother Kenyon, and Brother Vardell working him over on the ground. The plan of the old building was square, with four interior walls surrounding the yard; he entered through the heavy iron gate with bars, which he intentionally overly forcefully slammed against the wall, so the dull iron ringing loudly announced his arrival. It was a late April evening, it was quite late in the day, and it was already getting dark. The three young Mormons were standing on the other side of the yard; and he instantly got their attention. Everyone stood there for a few moments, Denis on one side and the Mormons on the other, wordlessly trying to make out each other's faces. When he decided he couldn't see well enough – it was too dark, and they too far off – Denis went closer. After a few steps, he first recognized Noah by the many pockmarks on his face, prominent lower jaw, and mouth full of white teeth. Brother Noah was from the same fucking town in Utah as Mary: they knew each other as it were from birth, their families were friends for years, and so it was him who was her chief defender. He didn't like her affair with Denis from the start, and although it was now once and for all over, it had lasted too long and he had put up with it only on her account. He, too, took a step towards Denis, while the other two stayed a little behind.

'Where is she? I wanna see her, Noah.'

They came to within a step of one another, and Brother Noah put a hand on Denis's shoulder, as if he wanted to confess to him.

'She's gone, Denis, she left the country. Believe me, it's better for both of you.'

'Well just go to hell! Don't you touch me with your homo hand!'

He used a backhand to knock Brother Noah's hand off his shoulder, then grabbed the Mormon by the shirt collar with both hands, pushed him aside, and headed towards the stairs that led to the upper floors, where the rooms were. Brother Kenyon and brother Vardell were still in his way; they signalled him to calm down and stop, not to go up. When he came right up to them, he did stop for a moment, gave them a friendly smile, and said, 'OK, OK', as if they had convinced him, but only long enough for the pleased Mormons to relax, and that's when he attacked. He tried to drive his forehead into Brother Kenyon's nose, but the 'Mormon asshole' managed to evade him some due to a momentary pause that was the result of Denis's inexperience with the move. So, Denis hit his lower teeth, which painfully dug into his forehead.

'Ahh, Dann.'

The blow to Brother Kenyon's head didn't put him on the ground because its inaccuracy robbed it of much of its potency, but it moved him aside enough that Denis could force the 'other pussy in a tie', Brother Vardell, to step aside with a kick ('There you go, a boot in your Mormon balls!') and slipped between the two towards the steps. When he had almost made it to the rooms, he felt a hand on his right shoulder that pulled him and turned him around. He saw Brother Noah, right hand clenched in a fist ready to fly into his face the next instant.

He had ridden to the main city park several kilometres from the North Side along a bike lane adjacent to the main road, which led by a huge, new, white marble office building that was erected several years before as some kind of declaration of change and the impending end of socialism. The comrades built it for themselves so it would be ready for them when they metastasized into *bona fide* gentlemen. The path continued by a large printing house and the municipal stadium; every other Sunday there were new and colourful urban tribes of soccer fans from Yugoslav cities large and small in the south stands, which had long been reserved for the fans of visiting teams who came to Ljubljana less and less to show their allegiance to their team and more to show they belonged to one of the newly awakened Balkan tribes. They were increasingly short of time to root for their team, because they spent most of it in street fights with the police and the not so numerous fans of the home team.

When he rode by the newspaper building and on into the railway underpass, Denis was very close to his destination, so he went ahead and lit a cigarette while still riding. Nor did he want to stop and turn on the bike's light, even though it was starting to get dark. The lighting on the main street was good enough, and the building where he was headed was right around the next corner.

Earlier in the morning that same day, he had gone through the same intersection in the opposite direction, from the police station to the North Side, on the back seat of the Lada Samara, with his old man and mum in the front seat. Both came to the station for him: his old man had the central, main role, and his mum was kind of in the background, like an extra. Anger and fear mixed on his old man's face, making him look a little confused, while his mum mostly sobbed. The police had brought him to the station, where the predictable course of events was more or less clear to Denis from the stories of friends who for one reason or another – mostly because of fights provoked by hot teenage blood and out of control hormones on Friday evenings – had turned up there. First, they stick you in a cell, where there's usually already some other teenager who won't end the evening with a *burek* at the bus stop, and some older drunk who went overboard, maybe spicing up his drinking with yelling hostile things about the system. When a certain amount of time passes – intended for you to lose whatever courage and resistance you came in with – and you feel the influence of the institution that makes you a little smaller, some junior officer in civilian clothes comes for you and takes you to an interrogation room, where you have to tell your story for the record, despite the fact that it's all crystal clear to him. Soon after making your statement, your parents come for you. They got a call in the middle of the night, and they were at first seized by the fear that something bad happened to you, but they're now seething with anger and can hardly wait to get home so they can start introducing completely new rules for your life, which they formulated in the car on the way to the station; even before that, your old man will give you a good whack by way of introduction, and your mum will be sure to say, 'Don't hit him over the head' although she'll fully approve of it.

Two boys of the same age awaited Denis in the cell that evening. They sat in silence and waited very peacefully, obviously accustomed to the surroundings and procedures. A frightened man of about forty sat on the bed in the corner, clearly finding himself in this situation for the first time. They apparently brought him in straight from the shop, because he was dressed in blue work overalls and his hands were black with grease. When the uniformed policeman closed the door, Denis's eyes rested on it for a while, as if he didn't yet want to be confronted by the co-sufferers waiting for him in the cell. He slowly ran a hand down the door. It was a real prison door of heavy iron with a small window for peering into the cell. He had to get up some courage to confront his gaol mates but finally did turn around, sighing a half audible, 'Ahh, mother fuck.' The boys only barely nodded a greeting, but the worker smeared with grease got up from the bed, marched over to him, and extended a hand.

'Drago, I'm Drago, my pig of a wife said I shoved her… Oh, the bastard, the bastard, what did she do to me!'

His eyes were red, as if he had just been crying, and he had unbelievably bad breath. Denis never smelled such a stench, but a year or so later, when as a member of one of the tribal armies he would talk with frightened prisoners, it would be very familiar to him. Then he would know that only human fear can stink like that. He didn't feel much like talking, so he only answered Drago's griping and cursing his much-maligned wife, with, 'Ah, fuck it, what can you say, it's useless to get worked up now,' then stepped past him, and chose a spot. When he sat down, he stared at his All Stars, from which they had removed the laces, and chewing his bottom lip tried somehow to recall the events that had taken place that evening.

The day that ended with Denis in a cell at the police station had begun flawlessly. Friday, sun, only a few hours at school, and then he was to meet Mary on Čop Street. At home he explained that he had things to do all afternoon in connection with preparing some ceremony, and that he would go out for a bit in the evening, so he would be tied up in town until one in the morning. When he was out Friday evenings with Peter or Goran, they always drank a bottle or two of cheap wine on the Ljubljanica embankment. It seemed like they had to: drunkenness and some other highs were things to be desired on Friday evenings. But this time he was enjoying sobriety, which enabled him to perceive pure, extremely sharp pictures of Ljubljana's old quarter, coloured by the warm light of an early spring sun – images with Mary's laughter in the background that were recorded on his hard drive like the image of careless youth, becoming more idealized with time; the colours increasingly warmer, the city more beautiful, the people walking about like extras in a film, happier, and Mary's laughter ever more prolonged. Her presence was enough, and he didn't feel the need to talk much, but she kept starting different, small conversations, as if she wanted to meet him anew each time.

'Why Lennon? Why not Jagger?'

'Don't really know, maybe because he's dead, death makes him human. Jagger on the other hand looks deathless, like a zombie.'

'So, you BELIEVE he died just to prove his humanity?'

'Nooo…'

He got angry that time, as always when he felt that Mary was trying to show that he and his friends believed or wanted to believe in something, despite the way they mocked every religion. He wanted to make a powerful impression on her with his poorly thought out ramblings that were really just hastily concocted notions.

'He died because that Salinger-reading idiot shot him in the lobby… But yes, death makes him human, just like getting old would. Those who don't get old or die, those are zombies, not people.'

Mary tried to decipher his digital code with ever new questions like these, as if from other worlds, and in his answers he would describe a person much like himself but with fewer flaws and fewer characteristics he wasn't proud of. And with more of the ones he didn't have but which seemed would suit him. Denis didn't ask Mary very much because answering her questions took up most of their time together, and perhaps he didn't desire additional information about her so as not to spoil the impression of perfection that he had formed about her.

'It's not really you that makes me crazy. It's the idea of you. The perfect you that my mind created is who I love.'

When he whispered that thought in her ear a few days previously, just after a kiss and before running for his bus, she didn't know exactly what to think. Her thoughts ran to taking offence and back.

So, that Friday was flawless before the event at the newsstand changed everything. The evening meeting with Peter and Goran at the Rio passed with casual fun. They drank beer and downed a vodka or two besides (Mary had juice), most of the time talking about EKV's new recording and smoking all the cigarettes they had. An hour before midnight, the old school waiters – white shirts, black vests, and bow ties – who served cheap alcohol to young alternatives while waiting for 'real guests' in the downtown tavern, locked the doors behind them. Peter and Goran set off looking for fun, which primarily meant female companionship, while Denis and Mary stood there for several minutes. She waited for him to show the way, and he crumpled up a soft pack of Winstons in his pocket after once again checking it was completely empty.

'Shit, I'm out of cigarettes.'

'That's all right, you smoke too much anyway.'

'C'mon, Mary,' he said with as wide a grin as possible, 'don't be such a Mormon and help me find some smokes.'

They first walked along Čop Street down to the Prešeren monument. There were only groups of teenagers, taxis, on-the-hour buses, and police patrols on the dim city streets at that hour. Only the dance clubs were open, with long lines in front waiting to get in. It didn't make sense to Denis to wait in line just to buy cigarettes. They set off towards the railway station, the only part of the city that was still open after ten o'clock. A little before Marx Park, a boy and girl with their arms around one another came towards them, each with a cigarette in hand, so Denis stopped them.

'Heh, hi, can you spare one please, I'm out, and nothing's open.'

The couple smiled meaningfully and looked at one another. 'Look, there's a newsstand open over there.'

They pointed at a newsstand several dozen metres ahead, from which a large patch of neon light was actually falling on the pavement. Denis looked at them questioningly, no newsstand was ever open at that hour, the two of them giggled as if they were high.

'No bullshit, pal, get your smokes there, and for free, it's open.'

The newsstand had indeed been opened, and not long before, with a brick or chunk of granite. The packs of Winston were more towards the back, so to reach them, Denis had to squeeze almost all the way in. The disapproval that Mary was clearly expressing pricked his conscience, too; he decided it would really be wrong to load up on whole cartons of cigarettes, but now, in a pinch, he would take just one pack, it wouldn't be a big thing. When he grabbed the red pack and was crawling out ('Do you need anything, Mary? A magazine, sweets, maybe chewing gum?'), the thuds of at least two pairs of feet could be heard coming from the park, which the thick crowns of high trees made darker than the surroundings.

'Oh, my God, Denis!'

'Stop, police!'

'Mary, run!'

Denis crawled out quickly, scraping himself on bits of broken glass, grabbed her hand, and they ran back in the direction of Prešeren Square; she followed him for a time as the two policemen's steps and cries grew nearer. He was fast enough to outrun them, because the cops had to hold their caps on their heads with one hand and use the other to keep aside their truncheons from between their legs. The rush of adrenaline only added to his speed.

'Eeeeh! I fought the law and I won, I fought the law and I won!'

Mary couldn't keep up any more, she let him go, her legs froze in fear of the police, who were getting closer, and she finally tripped and fell. He clearly heard her fall, looked back, slowed, and only said, 'Damn!' and waited for one of the policemen to run up to him, take him firmly by the waist, and lead him back to where his companion in blue was waiting with Mary. From the moment he looked back at her while running to the moment they separated them and took them in different directions at the closest station, on Trdina Street, where more than one hero of this Central European metropolis's nightlife had slept, they didn't take their eyes off one another. The whole time his look said 'Forgive me,' although there was nothing accusatory in hers. That was the last time he saw her, because several hours later she left the station accompanied by an official from the American consulate and the director of the closest Mormon mission. After that, she would quickly gather her things at the building by the central park and be on her way to Austria, where there was a larger mission and respect for the strict rules of mission life was more supervised.

Noah's words followed him, the ones he heard the moment they were uttered, but he was so focused on having to get into the building and find Mary that they didn't actually reach him. The line, 'She left the country,' hit him harder than Noah's fist.

# THE END

First, Goran stuffed himself into the narrow passage of the opening he noticed somewhere at the end of his suitcase. He had to crawl on all fours, squeezed hard by the walls of irregular shapes made from material he couldn't exactly define.

'Fuck, it's narrow. Like trying to stuff yourself into an asshole... without Vaseline. The fucking workers, I have to do everything for them. Damn, gotta replace them all with Chinese...'

The space was so narrow he had to bend his head, meaning he could only see his knees and nothing in front. So, after several tortuous minutes of crawling, during which he didn't even notice his expensive suit slacks being torn, he was surprised by the emptiness he flew through face first at the end of the passage and onto the hard asphalt. Before looking around and checking the condition of his teeth with his tongue and licking a drop of blood from a broken lip, he again cursed the boys in the shop who had arranged this adventure into the unknown for him. The dark side street where he was standing was unfamiliar. It certainly wasn't the company forecourt or anywhere nearby, where he might have turned up according to some sort of logic. If logic could exist after crawling through a secret passage out of a suitcase. Wherever he was, at least one thing was clear: he had managed to escape a lynching in the factory.

'Ha, ha, screw you! Screw you!'

He loudly yapped it up, with both hands giving the finger to the little air-hole from which he dove into the street, despite the fact it really was too small for such a thing.

'There aren't enough of you, not enough, you pussies!'

The loud echo of his yapping rebounded on his ears from the walls of the high rises and yanked him out of his euphoric excitement. He heard it echoing a few moments after he stopped completely and started looking around the small street, which could have been a side street in any city, a place for dumping rubbish out of sight, along with alley cats, homeless people, and other unsightly things. You can't recognize a person by his innards, and cities don't differ according to side streets like these. Goran hoped that the end of the street would offer an answer to at least one of the questions banging around in his head, as he prepared to navigate between the large, overflowing bins. Despite his certainty, the street did not open into some larger, illuminated street or square by which he might have been able to determine his location, but into another very similar small, dark street in which there was but a single bin, full of cardboard tents from which stuck out pairs of feet with shoes. Stepping over the sleeping homeless in his expensive clothes, quite raggedy from crawling out of the suitcase, and spotless, still shiny shoes, for the first time in a long time he felt as uncomfortable as when he came to practice straight from a meeting with marketing agents dressed in his father's old wine red double-breasted jacket, for which he received a hailstorm of jokes and laughter from Denis and Peter. He was also getting a little frightened. Everything he saw before him looked much like a scene from some filmed catastrophe, although none of the tall buildings that bordered his new world seemed to have been harmed in any way. So, it clearly wasn't an earthquake, fire, or maybe a flood, but judging by the number of sleeping bodies in the street that he was stepping over, like roots and bushes in a forest, he must have arrived in the middle of some unusual circumstances.

'And what the hell is this?'

He wasn't even close to the end of the street and couldn't see it – the street seemed quite a bit longer than the last one – when he felt a powerful grip on his right leg that was about to put him on the ground. Without taking time to think what or who was pulling him back, he tried with all his might to draw his leg forward in order to run, but it didn't work. The grip only tightened.

'Where do you think you're going in my shoes, you suit?'

Now he felt two hands pulling on him, and their grip was so firm that the leg on which he felt the full weight of a prone homeless body couldn't move an inch. He instinctively grabbed a nearby drum with both hands, turned around, and raised it high over his head, spilling black sooty dust over his head and back, then brought it down on the homeless person curled around his leg like an alley-cat with all his might.

'Get away, you fucking bum!'

The homeless man's firm grip loosened for a second only when he kicked him in the ribs with all his might. He took advantage of this to free his leg and run down the street, stumbling among the cardboard tents and sleeping bodies, who started to rise as he passed like grass after rain. As he ran, the dark blue tie danced over his face and he started to feel it was more than a totally unsuitable article from his wardrobe for this place and more like a noose around his neck that sooner or later one of the zombies chasing after him would latch onto, and so he quickly untied it and threw it away. He couldn't see the end of the street or an exit into another street where he could hide, so he just ran as fast as he could. He was always one of the fastest, ever since childhood, when he won cross-country races, and years of regularly running up and down a Golovec hill proved useful, so he knew they couldn't catch him. But he couldn't run forever.

* * *

The strong neon light blinded Denis, so he paused just before entering the space to let his eyes get used to it. The scene changed from a half-destroyed library and its dark stairway into a futuristic white space strewn with neon light and outfitted with narrow, almost invisible shelves of an artificial material on which rows of flawlessly arranged, brand new, shiny book spines (that one glance told you had never been touched) sucked in their stomachs and thrust out their chests. The books were snow-white, as if they were all part of the same large collection. The proud glow of the black letters that formed authors' names and titles attracted his attention. The space had the shape of a long tunnel that turned very sharply to the left some metres ahead. He couldn't see Azra, so he decided she was around the turn, but he couldn't simply pass by these flawless, new books without pausing for a moment to look at them after all those old books in the destroyed library. They were ordered by authors' name, but they were completely unfamiliar to him. He hadn't heard of any of them, although based on the number of titles under each of the names, he concluded that they were well-known writers, not novices. He went over their surnames: Hemon, Albahari, Štiks, Dežulović, Jergović... No, not one of the authors' names whose works were waiting for someone to take them off the shelf in the strange tunnel beneath the destroyed library meant anything to him. On the other hand, he thought, given the events of the past two hours, it would be strange if what he observed actually made any sense. Among the titles that flew by him as he slowly walked along the shelf, *Nowhere Man* in particular attracted his attention because of the Beatles' song, which he automatically started humming as he picked it up. When he got to the refrain and was just realizing with surprise that all the pages except the title page were blank, Azra spoke up.

'These are books whose time is to come.'

He saw the year of publication on the title page. 2002.

'2002?'

He raised his eyes, in which she could see surprise, fear, and a request for an explanation. She came up to Denis, stroked his face to comfort him, and took his hand.

'Come on, let's go, forget it. I want you to see something.'

He put the book back on the shelf and speechlessly let her lead on down the tunnel, the walls of which were stacked with books that were yet to come. A tense feeling that he was walking past books he would never read constricted his throat. Lately he'd been thinking of books he wouldn't get to read, the last time, the day the hick of a commander stuck the barrel of his rifle in his face, but before today he could only think of the endless number of books already written, whereas now all of the unwritten books were smiling at him from the shelves, which only increased the oppression. 'You're an impotent, you're some kind of impotent thing', the commander repeated like a parrot that day. He was a local 'hero' and got to be a commander without any real military training on account of his mercilessness to the enemy and the fighters in his unit who didn't try hard enough. Denis had once again set him off with his attitude towards his rifle, which was never clean, and he came up with an extra special explanation for reading instead of running the rag on a string up and down the barrel like the others, since it would be completely dirty again after the very next firing.

'Well, my rifle is the cleanest around,' was his answer to the commander's, 'Your weapon is dirty again, you little Slovene shit.'

He had a continuation prepared for his commander's questioning look, which he expected: 'It's not, fuck it, I didn't shoot anyone. It's clean, clean as a whistle.' When the vein on his commander's left temple bulged, known in the unit as the 'crazy vein', he knew that the rest of the conversation would be unpleasant, but he didn't expect to be looking at the (of course flawlessly clean) barrel of a loaded rifle up close in a matter of seconds. Despite the unpleasant situation in which his sharp tongue had once again landed him, he was still bothered by why his commander, who was already totally red-faced from yelling, called him an impotent. What did that have to do with anything? When he finally got a hold of himself, he couldn't help but growl, 'You mean potent? When you say impotent you really mean to say a potent thing?'

\* \* \*

While she was following the mysterious librarian between the book shelves along passages that were so narrow they had the feeling they were walking along the close, cobblestone street of an old Mediterranean town, Mary was watching yet another recording, one of Denis's last band practice, which she saw before being forced to leave the city.

**Recording 5**

It was a day when dark evening came too early because of an oncoming storm. Denis and the boys, who were already finishing practising in their shelter couldn't notice, but it seemed to her that it was she who opened the door to the dark atmosphere outside and let it into the poorly lit, smoky space. She was used to sitting down on the worn couch in the corner without a word and waiting for a break. This time, pointedly, none of the trio looked over at her. They were facing one another, each in his own corner, as if on the points of an imagined triangle, getting ready to play the next song. After the signal to start, Goran began beating a wild rhythm, which the short, cut-off riffs of Peter's guitar picked up loudly after several beats, and the whole thing sounded like some kind of counting, during which Denis, motionlessly fixed on some point in the triangle, calmly waited for his entry, following which the song shifted to a flowing, melodic part, when he would sing his verses, first in a subdued voice and then more loudly, none of which she could understand. She hadn't seen them play like this, angrily and yet unbelievably coordinated; as if they were fused by something, but at the same time wanting to hurl their best rendition so far, into each other's faces. Right after the loud ending, without even glancing at the other two, Denis unplugged his bass, put it on the stand, and approached Mary. First he said, 'Hi,' as he grabbed his jacket and cigarettes, then 'Let's go,' and disappeared out the door without saying anything to the other two. She stayed inside another unpleasant moment, caught Goran's accusatory and Peter's indignant looks, shrugged her shoulders in surprise, and said, 'Bye.' He was waiting at the exit, his jacket buttoned all the way up, hands in his pockets, and facing away from the building.

'What was that about? A fight?'

He nodded, his lips pursed, and when she questioningly raised her palms, he said, 'Fuckin' politics.' After that, they walked along in silence, and she asked him about the song they were playing. *'Krug'*, he said curtly. Although the word ['circle'] meant nothing to her, she didn't ask at the time what it meant.

The librarian led Mary through a labyrinth of bookshelves until they came to a door to some other room, where she paused for a moment. She smiled once more with her hand on the latch, then slowly opened the door and stepped out of the way.

\* \* \*

A scene from the film *The Firm* in which Cruise runs somewhere as fast as he can, nicely dressed – a real sprint down the street – came to mind. He imagined that he probably resembled him pretty closely, dressed up and running from a nightmare hovering behind him. 'Yuppy on the run.' Unexpectedly, out of nowhere, two hands appeared before his eyes, violently grabbed him by the collar, and dragged him aside, into a dark corner of the street. One of the palms covered his mouth and prevented the terrified scream surging from his lungs to blanket the street. He could hear the loud pursuit fall away, and he was left in silence, with the palm against his mouth slowly starting to release the pressure. His saviour had a black baseball cap on his head with a visor that covered most of his face. Without a word, he pulled him by the hand and led him back several steps, where he opened a sewer cover and motioned for him to go down. Goran had no choice but to trust him, so once more quickly looking around to check if anyone was watching, he lowered himself into the dark shaft. His saviour (or maybe it was a she?) followed and pulled the cover closed behind him so that it went totally dark.

\* \* \*

The wooded road that ever more steeply rose around the mountain suddenly ended before it brought them to any obvious goal. As if it were cut off. Peter stopped the car and, leaving two hands on the wheel, leaned forward towards the windshield, in which innumerable tall, dark green firs were reflected. He felt for the brake with his right hand, unable to grab it on his first try. When he finally pulled it, he slowly turned with a bit of a nervous smile towards his passenger, who opened the door without a word, got out, and hands on hips started to look around.

'Damn, I've had about enough of this quiet act' he mumbled to himself when he'd lurched out of the car. He pulled himself out with one hand on the door frame and the other on the roof. The presence of the attractive stranger was reason for him to tuck his shirt immediately back into his trousers, because it had been lifted far over his belly when he crawled out. Only then did he look over the roof to the other side, determined to demand answers; but she was no longer there. So, his, 'Listen,' which he'd intended as an introduction, flew off over the roof into emptiness, towards the wall of high green firs, instead of into the stranger's face. She was already far off: walking along a narrow path he only now noticed between the firs. 'Heh, wait up, for God's sake!' She didn't stop for even a second, nor did she look around, so he had to hurry after her. He tried to run, but immediately slipped and landed on his knees. Only when he caught up and started walking alongside did she direct a glance and a few words at him.

'A short walk in the woods will do you some good. And there's a surprise for you at the end.'

'Looks like a great gag, a wood, a mysterious woman in the middle of it, end of the road, don't know what it means exactly, and I've got work I'm now good and late for.'

'But you wanted to see Goran, right?'

She knew she would surprise him with that, but she didn't glance at him to see the surprised look when he stopped for several seconds and stared after her, causing him again to have to catch up. Even when he came alongside her again he kept quiet, although his chest was full of a nice load of juicy curses he could have rained on her right to the end of the narrow path, where a small wooden hut awaited them in the deep shadows of the firs.

\* \* \*

The tunnel she was leading him through had no end, neither did the rows of shining books he no longer dared to look at closely. Azra wasn't exactly the same as in the old destroyed library: she was somehow different. Her already light skin became even lighter, almost transparent. Perhaps the whole thing was due to the illumination. The light in the tunnel, which looked like a scene shot for a second-rate science fiction movie, was really strong, actually disturbing. But all the discomfort that had been building in his chest and throat disappeared, as if by a charm, when he entered the new space onto which she opened a door and let him through alone. Empty. The space was truly totally empty. That was the only word to describe it. Looking all around, he saw nothing but emptiness. Azra didn't enter. She closed the door behind him and he was left alone. He felt somehow more at ease, as if on entering he had shed a heavy suit of armour that had been boring into his shoulders the past year. He thought that if that was the end of his story, it was pretty poor, unspectacular; a little bizarreness by way of introduction, then emptiness, and that was it. Although the feeling was good, even sweet; like when after a long, hard day that won't end you finally fall into bed and contentedly give in for several moments before actually falling asleep. When the door again opened, he expected Azra, but a middle-aged man carrying a few extra kilos and noticeably thinning hair entered. With eyes wide open, just like Denis a few moments before, he first quickly sized up the space he had entered and then rested his eyes on him. By the surprise that lit up his face, Denis decided that the newcomer apparently knew him from somewhere, so he, too, looked at the other more attentively, but he recognized him only by the smile that spread across his face. 'Pero!' he wanted to cry ecstatically, but instead he only smiled and approached him slowly. Words, too, remained at the door like something unnecessary.

* * *

When Mary entered the empty space, all three were reunited: Denis, Peter, and Goran. She recognized Denis immediately, he was almost exactly as she remembered him, perhaps a year or two older and looking a little more serious, but still young (the first grey hairs she had recently noticed flashed through her mind at that realization). Of course, the uniform struck her as wrong. He didn't seem like someone who would wear it voluntarily. Goran was clearly older, but not so different that she wouldn't recognize him. But she only recognized Peter because he was the logical third in the group. They were standing like they were at the band practice where she last heard them play: Each in a corner of a small triangle that was now much smaller, its sides less than an arm's length. The silence that reigned in the empty space seemed unusually loud. As Mary approached them, the melody of the song they played that time still echoed in her head. They looked around when she took a step closer, as if they heard it, too. She stepped into what didn't happen. Like into some ending. Into the circle.

# AND AGAIN

Dear mum,

After all these years it's probably time I at least explain in a letter why I left the mission. Well, maybe I should say I escaped. In the middle of the night, in darkness and total silence interrupted only by the deep breathing of my roommates, I snuck off with my small backpack, barefoot, my All Stars in hand, on tiptoe. Only in order to reach out for the freedom that in the end I had to seize for myself around the first corner, where I put on my shoes. I didn't even say 'Bye' to any of the sisters, didn't let any of them suspect that I would leave, I didn't really feel any need to say good-bye to anyone. You know, mum, this feeling of not belonging is strange. Off hand, a person would say it's some kind of neutral, passive feeling that doesn't define you; you just don't belong to something, and that's that. How wrong, now that I think back on it, not belonging is exactly what defined me most deeply since I was small. All of that worshipping reserve and suppressing feelings that was preached at home, in church, and at school... 'Nope,' that was never for me, ever since I was small, inner emotional explosions shook me with destructive force. And then those books of yours... Yeah, your books, I can see you pretending not to know what I'm talking about (Disclaimer: as I'm writing these lines, I keep smiling at your embarrassment because you don't want to hear you're busted and busted big time, mum). Your books, but not the ones on the shelves in our house, precisely the same uniformed boredom you find on any shelf of any family like ours. I mean the ones you hid in the basement, in a hole in the floor, under the floorboards behind the washing machine. Are you surprised? I hope now that you know I know (if you still have any doubts, go back a few lines to the part where I make fun of your being upset), you're not thinking of acting ignorant and playing the roles you played all those years. I know. Accept it. And it was from that rainy day when I was thirteen (yeah, it's been going on that long and you know very well you weren't anything like the undisputed champion of pretence in our family), when instead of going to school I ran around the corner of the house. I went down into the basement through a window I opened ahead of time that morning, intending to hide there until the time I was supposed to come home. I knew that you would come to do the wash during the morning, so I prepared a hiding place in the old cupboard opposite the washing machine and fit myself in when I heard your footsteps on the wooden stairs. I thought you would just fill the machine and go back upstairs, so I wouldn't have to squeeze into the cupboard for long, because (as you yourself know well) it's small enclosed spaces I can't stand most, I have very morbid associations with them. In short, I was watching that rainy morning through the narrow crack between the cupboard doors. Even at moments when you thought you were completely alone in the house, that serious and somehow fed up with everything expression I was used to didn't leave your beautiful face. I always thought you were one of the most beautiful women I had ever seen, especially when you laughed, which unfortunately was so seldom that every such moment was impressed in my memory as a special thing. You allowed yourself a smile only when something (or someone) surprised you, caught you off guard, like the time father and I suddenly started beating each other with pillows (you remember? In the morning I snuck into your bed and five minutes later the room was full of feathers and a mix of a child's and a man's hollering (excuse all these parentheses, I can't follow my own thoughts without them, since they overwhelm me from all over)), so I couldn't even dream that on that rainy morning, hidden in the basement cupboard by the washing machine, I would catch one of your most beautiful smiles, on account of which I would never look at you the same way again. When, with rolled up sleeves and loosened buttons that revealed your full décolletage, into which a drop of sweat that crawled down your face and neck would disappear from time to time, you finally filled, closed, and started the machine, and instead of going back upstairs and saving me from being squeezed in the tight hiding place, you bent over behind the machine and disappeared from view for a few seconds...

And when you appeared again, preceded for an instant by cigarette smoke and the smell of hemp, you were no longer yourself. I saw before me a completely different woman with a small, narrow joint in one hand and a book that looked as if it had been read many times in the other. You sat down on a chair, loosed your hair from the ponytail so that it fell to your shoulders, and raised your feet onto the machine, letting your long skirt slide up your hips, fully baring them. God, how amazingly hot you were at that moment, mum, like Jane Fonda in Coming Home, free and sexy. You smoked the joint like some experienced hippy, using a wetted finger to make sure it burned evenly and holding in the smoke a long while after each drag, not once having to cough (now, as I recall it, that was the most fascinating part). Ah, I could hardly wait for you to go back upstairs so that I could rush to your hiding place, but you weren't in a hurry to go anywhere. Stretched out on the chair, your legs bared, three fingers gently coursing over them, with the joint between your index and middle finger, you gave the impression you would never go anywhere. You didn't read the book you had fetched from your hiding place. You only pulled from it a yellowed, densely lettered paper, obviously a letter. And while you were reading it, a smile that I had never seen before (and I don't remember if ever again) formed on your face. You were clearly pleased with the words your eyes followed over the yellowed sheet of paper, because you giggled like some embarrassed teenager. After reading it a long time, you carefully put the letter back in the book, which you let rest closed on your breast, and for a while just stared dreamily at the ceiling. You started and got up when the washing machine stopped. Your freely falling hair, that had been caressing your shoulders, was instantly gathered again into a ponytail and as if nothing had happened, you routinely went about your daily chores, a serious mask once again covering your face. When you finally left the basement, and I could get my numb limbs out of the cupboard, I went straight past the washing machine and impatiently crouched behind it. You had carefully camouflaged your hiding place, so I needed time to painstakingly examine each single piece in the wooden flooring in order to find the one that had to be raised. It took me several moments to get up the courage and reach for the pile of books that appeared. I pulled them out of the hole in the floor one by one and stacked them up. Even today, I remember each one precisely. The title, author, title page, and smell that wafted from the pages that rustled between my fingers. *To Kill a Mockingbird*, with a dark tree with white leaves, *On the Road*, with a girl sticking her head out a car window, *Franny and Zooey*, with two black and white faces, an ascetic *Catcher in the Rye*, with a drawing of Holden Caulfield in a red cap and cigarette in his mouth, not to mention... The letter you read was stuck in Kerouac's *On the Road*, at a page with text underlined in crayon or perhaps even dark red lipstick, which I of course never had the occasion to see on you: 'I was surprised as always, how easy the act of leaving was, and how good it felt. The world was suddenly rich with possibility'. The letter began, 'My darling', in handwriting other than father's ... Don't worry, mum, I didn't read on, I don't know why. I like to believe it was because, as a thirteen-year-old, I already had a fully formed opinion on not sticking your nose into other people's business, but I'm not convinced it wasn't a more banal and simpler lack of courage that stopped me from reading. On the other hand, I read again and again the underlined part of the text in the book. Leaving. The ease of leaving. The world's possibilities. From then on, those were the words to which I awoke and went to bed. Leaving, me leaving, was at first only a possibility I dreamed of. After a year or two of dreaming, it turned into the single purpose of my existence. As you see, despite everything, it was you who raised me. And not by the acting you staged daily upstairs, with you in the role of a quiet, dutiful housewife, but, unwittingly, by what you underlined in your books down in the basement.

It's an odd thing – freedom. A person can feel it in the most unexpected places, but on the other hand, be deprived of it in a place where people let the word roll off their tongues like something to be assumed. In Ljubljana, for example, which was for you and father a city on the other side of the Iron Curtain where there was state terror and no freedom, I met some people who might have been deprived of some things in life, but freedom certainly wasn't one of them, at least not then (the war that followed had a tendency to strangely influence people's inclinations). Whereas my life and the lives of other brothers and sisters at the mission were subject to countless rules (My god, there were more than a hundred and fifty of them!) and dreary daily routines (you must remember: be well kempt and clean, bathe often, use deodorant, exercise often, write a missionary diary) that permitted no deviations. Yet the young people we were vainly trying to sell on our truth to lived full lives without limits worth mentioning. They sat around in the parks, caught some sun on the river embankment downtown, slowly strolled the city streets and smiled as if they had all the time in the world. Yes, they smiled. Constantly, mostly without any cause. They smiled at one another, at passers-by, at their parents, and the police. Laughter is how we can identify a free person. And believe me, there wasn't much laughter among us at the mission. That's why without giving it much thought, instinctively, like someone who is drowning and just about to go under, I grabbed the hand Denis offered me to pull me out onto dry land, into a park, into the sun.

Denis? Now who's this Denis, I can just hear you asking. A young man. My boyfriend. At least he was for those few months before they dragged me off to some God-forsaken Austrian village. You know the feeling when you see someone for the first time in your life and you know right away. You know he's the one you've been looking and waiting for to hold your hand and take you away to all the places that were the real reason you left home. The whole time, my missionary work was a pretext, a possibility for escape, a small crack in the hard wall of the group rules that surrounded me since I was little – a crack through which I immediately escaped when the opportunity presented itself. Oh, mum, you should feel what I felt when I started breaking all those rules, one after the other. When Denis's eyes first met mine on the bus, I had already broken rule number 77 (don't flirt), a few minutes later, when he put his Walkman earphone spouting rock 'n roll to my ear, I broke rule number 41 (don't listen to unapproved recordings), and the same evening, when I went to a rock concert with him, rule number 75 (never allow yourself to be alone with a member of the opposite sex) and number 78 (don't go on dates). All of those broken rules fell from me like shackles to the Ljubljana streets Denis and I later walked so often, until the evening when everything went bad because of a single, instantaneous, wrong decision. I'm not going to bore you with the details, but Denis got into trouble he didn't need with the police, and that put an end to my stay in Ljubljana. Even later, when I left the mission, I didn't return, although I was tempted. First, I wasn't sure I even wanted to find out if we would be able to pick our relationship up off the street, like the old clothing the two policeman who chased us that evening tossed away; and when with the last breath of spring I finally decided that I had to find out, tanks roared up to the Austrian-Yugoslav border and shelling began, which you and father can follow even now (if, of course, you at least once in a while listened to the international news after I left). Instead of me leaving Vienna, where I was living, for Ljubljana, from that direction towards Austria and on to all of Western Europe there came hordes of mostly young people who wanted the normal, regular, and boring life they recently had but appeared to have lost irretrievably in the smoke of explosions, barricades, and snipers' shots.

Mum, after everything I've written, it must be clear to you I'm not coming back home, or at least not for some time. I'll keep travelling. Without a clear destination and schedule. Right now, I'm somewhere in Western Europe. I won't tell you the exact location, because I don't want you to look for me, it's enough that you know I'm nowhere near the war zones, so you don't have to worry. I'm fine, I'm working as a waitress, I have some small savings, and I'm thinking about enrolling in a course in the fall. I read a lot. You'd be proud of me. Since I work nights, I get up pretty late and spend my afternoons in the local library, which has a wonderful reading room. I really feel good there. There's a fascinating quiet. You only hear some careful, quiet steps and pages turning. I'm usually so immersed in reading that I don't even notice people in nearby seats. Last time a girl sat down next to me and attracted my attention. A tall, very beautiful brunette with short hair, she put a collection of Bruno Schulz's stories on the table in front of her. It was a small book embellished with the author's black and white drawings, self-portraits, and nudes. Heavy reading, honey, I thought to myself somewhat condescendingly; I hope you know what you're getting into and you perused Kafka before taking up Bruno. As if reading my thoughts, she turned to me and smiled, putting me in the somewhat unpleasant position of a voyeur caught red-handed. I tried to get out of it by pointing at the book in front of her and giving my opinion of it with a thumbs up. She nodded and started paging through it as if looking for something. She gave the impression of being familiar with it in detail, of knowing precisely where to locate the underlined passage she would show me in a moment. When she found what she was looking for, she turned the book towards me so that I could read the fluorescent orange highlighted text:

'His unlived life worried him, tortured him, turning round and round inside him like an animal in a cage. In Dodo's body, the body of a half-wit, somebody was growing old, although he had not lived; somebody was maturing to a death that had no meaning at all.'

Later, she told me her story in the library coffee shop, where she had invited me. She worked as a librarian in a small Bosnian town until the night the hostile army's soldiers marched in after a long siege. The next day, they loaded her and the other women into the old white city buses that hadn't burned in the barricades into which the town's defenders had shoved all the other vehicles. The men were made prisoners in the school gym where a few years before they played basketball, handball, or volleyball with some guy who now guarded them. Her last look at the town that day was from a rise on which a pair of howitzers, that had spread fear and panic in the town the past several nights, were still dug in. All of the women on the bus stared silently through the large back window, which like a full-sized television screen framed the panorama of the town, in the middle of which, like an open wound, gaped the roofless library. She said that from a distance it looked like the Barbie house her father had brought her from Trieste years before. Loud yelling to the left of the bus roused them from their stupor. Apparently, a fight had erupted among the soldiers guarding the position with the two howitzers. They saw how one, to judge by the markings on his uniform perhaps even the commander of the small unit, was pointing the barrel of his automatic rifle at another, younger soldier. There was no fear to be seen on the latter's face, only ridicule. The bus didn't slow down, it kept on, so the scene with the fighting soldiers rushed by their eyes too quickly to see how it ended. The woman was sure she heard the sound of a shot several seconds later. Just one, and then silence again. She dispensed with the sense of instantaneous pity she felt at the vivid image of the feisty young face falling into the mud at his commander's feet with the rational explanation to herself that he was one of the enemy who was to blame for all her misfortunes and those of all the other women on the bus, and the fact that the aggressors had started killing one another ought instead to make her happy. But she kept visualizing the scene and when later she read the passage from Schulz that she showed me in the library, it spoke to her exactly about him, the young man right before his death talking back to the goon with the automatic rifle. She even had vivid dreams about him the first night she spent in a foreign country: unusual, bizarre dreams. They were in her roofless library, it was night, and all of her co-workers were still there, even those who she hadn't seen for a long time because they were drafted. When she described him to me, how careful he was with the books in the library and how he strove to win her over, which he managed to do in the end by singing some well-known song, I thought, 'My God, that could be Denis.' Although it seemed so unlikely, after that coffee in the coffee house of a modern library in a Western European city, I stopped thinking about returning to Ljubljana. Of course, that day I went home with my own copy of Bruno Schulz, who shared a fate similar to that of the soldier in the young Bosnian woman's story. Perhaps you'll also include Schulz in your 'basement collection'?

Well, that's enough for now, maybe I'll even send you the letter and maybe another one some time. For now, give dad a kiss and take care of yourself.

*Love, Mary*
*Europe, autumn 1995.*

My Dear Denis,

I don't know where you are or even if you still are, but I felt a terrible urge to write you a letter. A real one, on paper, and by hand. Since I've been writing exclusively at a keyboard, my handwriting is semi-illegible. I'm no longer able to write five sentences with a fountain or ballpoint pen that I would know myself how to read reliably. Sometimes, when you were still around, I copied whole collections of song lyrics with chords without having to go back and correct even one word. Just a while ago I was straightening out the drawers and found one of them. The writing was legible, as if it weren't mine, no corrections, no crossing out at all, and fewer mistakes than you find in printed books nowadays after they supposedly passed the editor, proof reader, and the rest. We've simply become careless, we don't like to put real effort and work into anything, we're not prepared to devote the time needed so that what we create, write, compose, or fashion is something really worthy of note. We appear to be dissatisfied with everything, we criticize everything, but in fact it's the opposite: everything passes. All kind of crap, whether a poem, a book, a film, or other, more serious things – it's all good enough to pass. You wouldn't believe what a poor excuse for a society we've become, when the first several years it seemed we were like a rocket shot into the sky, flying much faster than others, especially than those down south, where I suspect you are, where they were hunting and killing each other. What a person like you is to do in such a situation exceeds my imagination. You probably couldn't join a band, although we also hear romantic stories about how in basements and shelters they played music, put on plays, watched films, had entire fucking basement film festivals, and how people didn't lose their sense of humour even at the worst times in Sarajevo and other places that were shelled and under threat of bombings. Here we like to believe such stories, because they ease our guilty conscience somewhat for having stood by and acted as if those were some faraway countries, fucking Iraq and Iran or Lebanon and not parts of what until yesterday was our country. And now that the shooting's over, crowds of us head south, as if on a safari, to search for something that is long gone. We search for Bosnians, but we find only Muslims, Croatians, and Serbs, we search for Bosnia, and we find only the Federation, Hercegovina and the Serb Republic. The Bosnia we're searching for is nowhere to be found. When there was still shooting down south by you (You're still there somewhere? I suppose that if you left the country, you would have been in contact on the way. Or am I mistaken?) we were living our dream of a successful small country, an Alpine paradise. They really put one over on us. While we were happy about the new shops, the cars on credit, and the cheap airline tickets, THEY erased you and people like you, and stole a little on the side. Well, in fact it was more than a little. Who are THEY, you ask? THEY are... how to explain it to you? Let's try this way. A while ago I read Haruki Murakami's novel *A Wild Sheep Chase* (by the way, if you haven't read it, his *Norwegian Wood* is a *must read* for a Beatle maniac like you). In the novel, Murakami plays with the idea that somewhere high up in the snowy Japanese mountains there is a metaphysical sheep that is the source of political, and thereby social, power, that he temporarily confers on one and then on another individual. Each recipient is strongly convinced that he is the source of the power, not knowing that it is conferred on him only temporarily and that when it leaves him what awaits is the curse of eternally searching and yearning for what he once had. So, who are THEY is the wrong question, because THEY are only temporary recipients of the same power or control that Party members once had. Maybe they are some new faces in new pseudo-democratic dress, but the power by which they decide my and your (especially your) fate is precisely the same as the one that decided the fates and lives of our fathers. I digress. Let's leave aside society and politics for now; first let me tell you about myself, although the story has a very similar arc.

It's funny to write a letter to a friend you haven't seen or heard from in more than fifteen years. It's as if writing back into the past. You're still there somewhere in the early 1990s, nineteen years old, as you were when I last saw you, and I'm close to forty and have become a very sad, unfortunate, and pale copy of the Pero you remember. Every morning in the mirror I seem a shade older and fatter and a bit more of a drunken loser than when I left here the evening before. It's no surprise that Tanja took off, I would, too, in her place. I even think she held on too long. In the end, the last several months, I bet myself when would be the day of her departure. Depending on the bet, I would even do extra to encourage it, or by all means try to prevent it. So, one day I offended and aggravated her, behaving like the biggest chauvinist pig, and the very next day I was a pleasant, polite lapdog full of apologies and promises. It's no wonder she was confused. I now truly hated her as much as I once loved her. But she wasn't guilty of anything, she was simply too close to me, so close that she could observe my transformation from a somewhat promising student into a drunken, fat bureaucrat who could be glad that no one in the civil service really likes to deal with redundancy; all the same, everyone there is making a good show of it on taxpayers' money. And she, as if she wanted to fuck with my head even more, remained the same excellent person she was in college, when we met.

She studied Italian and French, but I don't know which was her major and which the minor. We met at some mini event in the department, where a high school acquaintance had invited me to play Jacques' Brel's *Ne me quitte pas*. She set up a meeting with some Tanja, who was supposed to bring me her mum's LP with the song on. We were supposed to meet after her classes at seven in the evening in front of the drama theatre. She was a little late, so I could observe her from a distance as she approached. I couldn't be sure it was her, but I asked God for it to be, because, take my word, she looked excellent. A beret, long blonde curls, scarf, miniskirt, and tall boots, as if Nancy Sinatra herself were walking in my direction. I was all worked up even before she introduced herself. 'Tanja.' 'Pero.' 'I guess you need this old record.' Fuck, what a smile. 'I guess even you students of French are hot for Jacques.' I was no slouch either. Then. I returned the smile, which was supposed to communicate something like, 'You're cute, hon, you might even interest me if you try.' Go ahead and laugh, I was pretty successful with that pose for two years in college. 'I guess today's philosophy students aren't familiar with him' (she meant Brel, in case you lost the thread). 'Too bad.' She pulled the record out of her bag. On the cover was the yellowish face of someone who could have been, depends how you look at it, an uglier Belmondo or the more handsome brother of Shane McGowan, with a pure white cigarette in his mouth, which couldn't be anything but Gitanes (you remember how we almost coughed up our lungs on them when Goran swiped them off his dad and brought them to our place), the fucking motherfucker, in short, as if cut from some film noir. 'But will you be able to play the piece? I mean since you don't know French?' 'If I could play Carlos Pueblo without a day of Spanish, I can do this Frenchy. But I could probably use a little help with the gurgling. Maybe you could tutor me?' We got together at her place two days later. A large flat in old Ljubljana, full of paintings, books, and old records. It looked like her old man was some heavy hitter. I already knew the piece, I practised it and analysed it for two days, I wanted to be as ready as possible to visit Tanja, to knock her off her feet with the first rendition. But she wasn't easy. She took her time. She stopped me and corrected every other word, explaining their meanings, how they're pronounced, the position of the tongue (that got me even hotter), so that after two hours I was completely worn out. At a certain point she finally stopped talking, and let me sing the whole song for her, and somewhere towards the end, when my playing changed from slow and melancholy to a little more rhythmic and loud, she started rubbing her bare heel against my calves, so that

I swear my Levis were going to split from the pressure. I could hardly wait for the end of the song so that I could put aside the guitar and jump her. We went down right there, in the living room. An excellent start and such a sorry, pathetic ending that I'd rather not describe it to you at all.

I don't see Goran much. Even in college we were seeing less and less of each other. You probably remember that the economics department is north of the city, far from the humanities downtown. Probably so they don't infect each other. The more I think of it, that's perhaps the root of all our current problems, the great distance between the humanities and economics. However that may be, Goran always played on the winning team. On the team with people who took for themselves everything they wanted and now have much more than they need. Based on what I've written so far, it's probably not necessary to explain that I'm not even close to being part of that team. After graduation, Tanja and I took a small van that was fixed up in some dubious garage, on a trip across Europe, which later turned out to be a sort of advance honeymoon. That's because one evening not long after we returned, Tanja came crying from the bathroom with a Clear Blue stick in her hand. Two parallel blue lines laughed at me and my desire for an extra, carefree year to do either post-grad studies or make music. They nixed all my plans and plan one became the arrangement between my mum and Uncle Stane for me to intern in the Ministry of Culture after graduation. The moment I passed through the door to my first, and until now only job, is like the highest point in a ride at the Luna Park, after which the next second you plunge down at a speed that only increases by the minute. Every day I could observe different phases of my coming decline in the ministry offices I passed on my way to the little closet at the end of the hall. In one sat 35-year-old Brane, who was going through divorce proceedings and hardly did a thing but argue on the phone with his wife, who wouldn't allow contact with the child or her attorney; she accused him of doing nothing but flaunting his incompetence. Next came 55-year-old Dušan, who used most of the day planning his bike training and marathons; 55-year-old Jelka, who was just recovering from a big operation, waiting for the medical results, and mostly crying; forty-year-old Jurij, who spent entire days on top-notch PowerPoint presentations the cretin thought would impress the teacher of his seven-year- old daughter, for whom he'd wait for an hour and half in front of the Pioneer centre, where the little girl was already learning English so she could impress the teacher she'd have in two years. And so on past countless offices stacked on several floors of the ministry building. Total bureaucratic hibernation broken up by weekends, holidays, and vacations. I could hardly wait for the lunch break to drink a large bottle of Union beer, which relaxed me enough to allow me to hibernate the rest of the workday. I increased the daily dose with the years from two or three, now in the morning, besides smokes, I buy a small bottle and a pack of Wrigley's gum, the one with the strongest flavour. It's sad, I know. I know that you'd drag me off somewhere where I would have to say to people sitting in a circle, 'I'm Peter and I'm an alcoholic.' I'm really sorry I didn't try harder to find you.

I only looked for you in my dreams, always the same ones that I dreamt over and over: I'm travelling south on a train, to Bosnia, where your grandmother lives, which offers me the only orientation for searching. In the compartment are five guest workers who are going to take a break from slaving away in the Alps. The five talk a little before going to sleep, not looking at each other much, since they're together the whole day on the work site and then in the evening in rooms smaller than prison cells where their owners accommodate them. They can barely wait to get out and disperse to their homes so as not to even hear of each other for several days. I can't go to sleep, so I go out into the corridor to smoke. I blow smoke through the half-open car window across which the shadows of mostly empty houses fall, and listen to the train's blues rhythm. Ta-dam-ta-dam, ta-dam-ta-dam, ta-dam-ta-dam. A constantly uniform, monotonous, and perfect rhythm, as if the bluesman John Lee Hooker were playing on his porch, reclining in an old rocking chair. I think of all those empty villages in the middle of that God-forsaken place that the only people prepared to live there had already fled, and which was now waiting for some fictitious, non-existent members of the enemy tribe to settle there. Meanwhile the fences are rusting, the walls are crumbling, the roofs are falling in, grass and weeds cover the stone paths that bear the impressions of many generations' countless footsteps. As I'm thinking this and pressing the butt into the ashtray by the window instead of flicking it out, a compartment door opens at the other end of the car, on my right, and a woman steps out. Long, dark hair covers her face when she looks down and searches the leather bag slung from her shoulder. She looks attractive and is certainly better company than the five sniffling Bosnians in the compartment, so I decide to light another cigarette to justify my distant presence in the corridor. I open my lighter at the same moment the woman opens the window in front of her so that the wind starts to part her hair and I can clearly see her face for the first time. Fuck, I can't believe it. 'Mary?' 'Mormon Mary, is that really you?' I walk towards her down the long carriage, and she looks at me totally calmly, as if it's the most normal thing in the world for us to meet here in the middle of a train scene, winding through the Bosnian hills on an autumn night on its way from Germany to Sarajevo. As awkward as I am, I extend a hand to shake, but she gently puts a palm on my neck, pulls me close, and kisses me. Long after, when we're sitting and relaxing and chatting on the rug on the carriage floor (the conversation is now somehow off and inaudible), I feel the touch of her palm on the back of my head and the press of a kiss on the cheek, warmer than one you'd expect between friends. It's a cold, foggy morning outside when we get off the train. We take a taxi to the village, an old white Mercedes with a leather wrapped steering wheel. When we go into the garden, your mother appears at the door of the house. She is dressed in black. This is where I usually wake up. Except once, when I dreamed on – we were in a small, cheap hotel room near the train station, Mary's sweaty body entwined with mine...

Hmm, I believe you're now surprised. 'What?' you think, 'you and Mary?' I'd like to write I have no idea why, but fuck it, I damn well know the reason for her presence in my dreams. I was crazy about her when she was with you. Totally fucked up, nuts about her. Of course, you didn't notice anything, because you, too, had eyes only for her when she was around and I didn't register at all. When she sat in our place and listened to us practice, I played only for her, without her knowing it. But she had eyes only for you and ears only for your voice, she didn't notice my efforts. In those rare and brief moments that you disappeared from the stage, I hungered like a starved dog and tried to make the most of them. No, don't worry, nothing happened between us, I knew that because of you I didn't have a chance, but simply the possibility of a brief, private conversation with her was priceless to me. A smile or some friendly banter was enough for me. After they threw you out of the country, I even tried to find her in Austria, but with no success. When I went to the Mormon headquarters there, they told me that I missed her by several weeks, that she had disappeared without a trace one night, leaving only Jack Kerouac's *On the Road* on her bed, opened to a page with this text underlined with lipstick: 'I was surprised as always, how easy the act of leaving was, and how good it felt. The world was suddenly rich with possibility.' I knew she didn't go back to America, that she was somewhere close by, but I didn't look for her any more. The way she left was only more proof that you two were made for each other, which doesn't mean, of course, that you will ever actually be together. The opposite is likely. Because life is a merciless, manipulative bitch.

Tomorrow I'm going to the basement. Your bass and my guitar are stored there. I'm going to dust them off, change the strings, and test them. Maybe I'll play a piece. Maybe I'll even call Goran and get together with him for a drink. I'll convince him to drive to your grandmother's village and try to find out about you, although I'm sure we won't find you, not there or anywhere. The world wouldn't be the way it is today if we had you, Milan and Megi from EKV, and some others who burned out in that incomprehensible time. Despite that, I've known for a long time that I have to make that trip someday. Maybe I'll find an answer for myself too. I need it, believe me.

All the best, old buddy, wherever you are.

*Your Peter.*
*Ljubljana, today.*

Pero I'm typing you this on my blackberry mini keyboard as the next part of our conversation yesterday. I'm afraid it might be time to take stock, that it'll ✉

sum it all up and we'll figure if it's a win or it sucks. That's what it's about in the end, no? In the end you figure the winners and losers. If I'd have summed it up two hours ago, ✉

before the guys on the shop floor decided to make a fucking revolution, there wouldn't have been any doubt: I would've been the clear winner. Winner of what? ✉

Winner of what, I can just hear you asking cynically. Of fucking life what else ☺ Like that squirt DeVito would say in *Other People's Money*: who has the most when he dies, ✉

wins. And I have the most in this company. MOST! Even more than that old fart Stepinšek ☺ I fucked him over too. If he gave a fuck, he'd have learned English when he had the time, ✉

and he wouldn't have had to go through me to work things out in Lichtenstein. I faked the papers so the old guy thought he was the hidden owner of the offshore company. Hidden dick more like, ✉

Goran's not a dope to stick his neck out for others, for that cretin son of his to screw it all up when his dad kicks it. I know, right now you'd give me that ✉

moralizing look of yours and try to prick my conscience, but even if I think it all through, there's no regrets, I'd do it all exactly the same. But ✉

even better ☺ Anyone would. Even you, you fucking straight Pero would do the same if you had my brains and especially my balls. And every one of those blue aprons down there who are crying now ✉

about how they were wronged. The only wrong I can see really happened to them was they were born dumb and incompetent. OK, I admit it, nature ✉

is a bitch, gives to one but not the other, but why should I have a bad conscience about that my whole life and pretend to be some socially conscious self-denying type and ✉

not buy a car I like and not have a great time and food at fancy restaurants instead of at some cheap dump and drink Ballantine instead of Lagavulin and not fuck young pussy, which ✉

likes all of this (and yeah, to be clear: I don't give a fuck if they're dumb, that's just your only comfort 'cause they don't like you with your gut and pie in the sky). That's the way the world ✉

is nowadays fuck it: the smart ones take money from the dumb. And thank god there's never a shortage of dumb people (if you think about it there's always more), there's all the moolah you can want for us ✉

smart ones. Of course you'll say that's dishonest or that's immoral and us clever ones should set limits and not take every cent we can. ✉

Maybe that's even true but not on account of your moral ethical bullshit that always gets on my damn nerves, but 'cause of a much simpler ✉

practical reason: 'cause it never occurs to those cretins down there they also got their trump cards they can use to fuck every one of us clever guys... ✉

Funny, no? You're kinda wishing this situation on me, rooting for the workers, you're glad for them, you think that after all these years of us stealing they're like ✉

morally justified fucking with us a little, right? OK, to be real honest I admit it: at root there's no difference between what they're doing now and what ✉

we did to them. And if I'd tell them right now in our old neighbourhood with the street pride I still got in spite of everything: OK boys you won fair and square, ✉

you finally did it, only fuck it... not really. I mean won. They didn't. Why? 'Cause of all those vehicles with spinning blue lights that are ✉

parked all around the factory and the robocops inside ☺ ☺ In the end they'll go in and announce closing time like the blue shirts in the Lunov Magnus comics. And since they probably weren't even close, ✉

when we clever ones went on the offensive ☺. In the end we'll still win, long live the cops! So again: get fucked Pero with all your moralizing ✉ that still amounts to saying between the lines that you don't have the balls to shove it in my face and tell me what you've been thinking for fifteen years: that I'm a phony punk idiot without ✉

any feelings who has trouble with foreign and long words and that it's an eternal wrong that all those fucking fat books didn't help you from becoming a drunk loser, ✉

whose own wife couldn't stand looking at any more much less fuck, and she found a younger asshole prospect. Oops... heh, sorry, Pero, for that. ✉

That was really low, I can't erase it 'cause I already sent it. The stress or something is fucking with me, sometimes I'm a real cretin. Tanja's really a cool woman and I always liked ✉

her, although I know I got on her damn nerves and I know she tried with you longer than any other would. But you, you turned into something totally different ✉

the past few years. You even got on my nerves. I don't know if the alcohol is fucking with you or something else (there has to be a reason for the alcohol, no), I really couldn't take you anymore. Damn ✉

when I remember what a cool guy you once were and what a great couple you and Tanja were (so that there were times I was jealous of you on account of her, not in a bad way) but really ✉

sincerely I was jealous of the life you two had ahead, although it was nowhere near as wild as mine ☺ I would've liked to smack you. Really. How could you ✉

fuck it up so splendidly? Damn, when you got something, you take care and add to it (at least that's my phony business logic) you don't piss it all away. And for what? ✉

For what? 'Cause you didn't realize yourself as a fucking musician? Or 'cause you didn't realize (am I using the word right?) yourself as a philosopher or go to work at that ✉

worthless university of yours? Fucking realizing yourself fucked you up, life is a lot plainer than you and the likes of you think it is. You're born, you put on your shorts, you ✉

play a little, then you party and fuck some, study and fuck a little more, work way too much and try to party and fuck some more, then you can't fuck any more and you start to ✉

eat and drink well, then you can't eat and drink well any more and you start to tell everyone around what to do, which is kind of stupid since you're 80 and you've got a nappy on your ass ✉

'cause you started to shit and piss in your shorts again and for ten final years nobody at all is sorry for you (because you sucked so much blood and time from those close to you in recent years ✉

that your biting the dust was a salvation) in the silence, unaware of yourself and your life, because dementia finally set in ✉

you croak. And that's that, nothing spectacular just a fucked up senseless life like a billion others. And most accept it and try at least to get max pleasure in ✉

while it lasts. Only imaginative shitheads like you muck it up and look for some deeper meaning and harass people around them. Take Denis for example. What ✉

kind of fucking deeper meaning did his life have? You're walking down the street with two friends, and two pigs on a routine patrol grab you and throw you the fuck out of your own life into some ✉

fucking surreal (how about that word ☺) war and then some shepherd that doesn't understand shit, that doesn't realize that you're from somewhere else, that somewhere else there's a band waiting for you and even some ✉

other life of yours that's on standby, you take a bullet, the end. *Ende. Finito. Vege.* So what's the difference between you and the rabbit happily hip-hopping through the grass, ✉

when this wasted guy comes by in a green uniform and sprays a fistful of lead up his ass? No difference, or some. None. In the end there's no prize and no punishment ✉

thank God (there's an internal contradiction in the sentence, don't you think ☺) except maybe regrets in the final moments when a guy might say to himself: why didn't I… ✉

I don't know… do something more often if I liked it so much. So you see, that's why I always absolutely always do exactly what I like in the moment and take ✉

exactly what I can get in the moment, whether that's a car, a watch, a stereo, food, drinks, or some pussy so my last thought in life won't be: damn why didn't ✉

I… let's say: why didn't I the time that I was offered my first fucking white line and ✉

try it, it's excellent, and why after I tried it didn't I stop or at least do it more prudently, so at moments I wouldn't feel completely fucked up and it seemed to me ✉

such mindless things were happening that Kafka would have a hard time following (it was him who wrote that short, thank God, story where this guy wakes up and he's an insect)? ✉

so that when I thought about whether those things really happened (even though I got them recorded on my fucking hard drive) I was actually still confused and fucked in the head. But ✉

let's forget about that, I can't type any more on these crappy small keys, and it gets on my nerves, really gets on my nerves when this fucking blackberry keeps cutting me off at only 160 fucking characters. ✉

Know what I think? It would be cool if some orgasmic force brought us, me, you, and Denis back together for at least a moment, for at least a fucking moment… ✉

'dio pal, hang in there LPG

Pero and Goran,

Yesterday I read in a newspaper several weeks old that was opened on the floor of an empty house at the beginning of a village we were combing for possible snipers, that EKV's Milan Mladenović died. The piece was short, as if it was about some old, long-forgotten partisan memoirist, but the local branch of the partisan's union placed the obituary, so the editor couldn't say no but gave it three skimpy lines on the edge of the page. There was no photo, so at first I thought it was probably a coincidence, there are any number of Milans and Mladenovićs here. But as I was standing there looking through the sights of my rifle and in the fog of indecipherable tiny text saw the letters E, K, and V, I knew. At that moment I was an ideal target for a sniper: focused on the crumpled and stomped-on page of an old newspaper, in a strange living room in which an Iskra television sat on a faded old table. As soon as the house was inspected and deemed clear, one of my 'comrades' would liberate it and put it in the trailer. As for myself, I always enter other people's houses, and especially their living rooms, somehow humbly and respectfully, as if going into a church or cemetery. You can't imagine how incredibly large I am when I'm standing in full battle gear somewhere between the couch and television, at the middle point of a living room. Like Gulliver in the land of the Lilliputians. I think about how several months ago, when my brothers-in-arms and I were still far away from this town and unimaginably abstract to its residents, a whole family would sit down in the evening in this tight space, together with grandfather, to judge by the brown walking stick leaning in a corner, and watch television together. As the oldest, grandfather probably sat in one of the easy chairs and got a little angry at certain scenes, which he didn't really understand, father snoozed in another after a hard day's work in the nearby foundry and afternoon odd jobs to supplement his miserably low pay, and mother certainly sat on the edge of a chair she brought from the dining table and put between the living room and kitchen so she could help her husband, father-in-law (was grandfather her father?), and children, if they needed anything. At the same time she was close to the stove, so she could throw an extra log on now and then, and the kitchen, where she was baking *pita*. The two children (I suppose they were son and daughter) were lying on either side of the couch, sometimes quarrelling and kicking one another when one felt that the other had stuck a leg over the imagined line that divided their territories. That is, a family like any other, with its usual, peaceful, almost boring life, the traces of which I can see all over the house, having broken in uninvited. The blue work jacket on a hook behind the door, a pair of worn women's shoes with low heels, and a pair of grey knock-off All Stars. Opposite is a broken mirror that holds countless images of the family members, who day after day, month after month, year after year looked into it just before leaving for work, school, or the market, and straightened their jackets, tucked in their shirts, carefully fixed their hairdo, and straightened their eyebrows with wetted fingers... It probably holds their last images as well, one after another, each family member separately. That time they all passed by the mirror as if it wasn't there, without looking into it, dressed in warm winter clothes because they didn't know where they would be in the evening and even where they would be sleeping in the future, hurrying, each with his own little suitcase, because we were practically in the town already, and they looked back at the living room for the last time, where I'm now standing like a giant foreigner, still smelling their fear and the scent of the last coffee that mother made them on the white wood fuel range, just like the one my grandmother has in the upstairs room of her house. The last one to leave the house, only father looked into the mirror. He was in a cam-ouflaged uniform, just like the one I'm wearing, only the stripe above the elbow on his right arm was a different colour than mine, but to the colour-blind they're the same grey. (Fuck, if everyone had Daltonism, if they couldn't distinguish colours, couldn't they patrol these damn hills together?) He had to pause for a moment at the sight of his own uniformed image, and when he turned to leave, he took another look and angrily hit the mirror with the butt of his Kalashnikov, exactly the same as mine, and it broke into six pieces of very different sizes, which the frame still held together. It was as if he wanted to be sure that over all the images of his family it fixed mine and those of everyone who came after me to carry away the television. He didn't want it to fix the image of the one who would put a flexible detonating wick into a dark green twenty-litre canister of gasoline and, when he was a safe ten metres from the house, toss down the match he used to light a cigarette. Yeah, the house will go up in flames, I already know that. It's always that way.

Reading these lines, you're probably surprised, and you can't really understand who this person is who's writing to you. Don't worry, it's still me, only I've adapted some to the circumstances. Like a salamander. I hope you're doing well and that at least you two are living a logical continuation of the life we had together. Pero, plug in my bass once in a while and play some song every – no, you know what, sell it, no, wait, even better: give it to some new kid who wants to join a band, and let him proudly take it to some shelter or garage. There's no sense keeping it for me, because I won't be back, I know. Even if I save my hide, even if the bullet with my name on it doesn't find me (you remember, don't you? I'm sure that at this point you're both thinking of Baldrick in *Blackadder*, how he engraves his name on a bullet so he has the one with his name on it on him), I can't imagine returning. The morning the police drove me from Ljubljana to the border it seemed that all of you who were staying looked the other way. If when my old man and mum were leaving, the neighbours covertly watched from behind the curtains and maybe even had a bad conscience, that morning it seemed that no one, absolutely no one in the whole city was even watching as I left. No one looked around at me for even a second, to tell the truth it seemed like the entire time I saw only peoples' backs on the streets. It wasn't the same city, it wasn't a city I would want to go back to. My city was no more, just as this town no longer exists for all those people who fled before us, they took it with them and left us only its shell, for us to rummage around in like stray dogs looking for... looking for... What are we looking for?

I often dream of Mary. Who was she really? A Mormon? Sure. Was her dropping into my life really just an accident without any connection with what happened later? I'm more and more sure it wasn't; that she had some role. Maybe she was a temptation I had to resist, let her pass by, tie myself to the mast. But, heh! Did I actually have a choice? The force with which she attracted me the instant I first saw her on the bus was unbelievable, I never experienced anything like it before or after. Yeah, Goran, I know what you'll say. 'Yoko Ono, the woman who ruined it all.' But is that true? Should John have avoided her and left the Indian's gallery as if nothing had happened and gone back to Paul in the studio to write yet another genius song? And another one after that. And another. And another. In the end the whole thing would have become routine, genius in their case, but still routine. Routine is warm and safe, it means driving on cruise rather than jumping into the unknown, not knowing how far down in empty space you'll find the first solid purchase, how long you will simply fall, dizzy with emotions, adrenaline shooting into your veins like out of a sports car's fuel injectors (Goran, forgive me if the comparison isn't the most appropriate, you know that I actually have no idea what different parts under a car's bonnet do). And there will be days when you're sure you're on top of the world and like a black and white James Cagney you'll yell at everyone else down below, and right after that there will be days when you can't stand yourself, when you'd rather just snap at those closest to you, because they'll get on your nerves, because they'll be guilty for you falling in a hole. If you're the Beatle named John, you don't have a choice. You jump.

I often think about practising, too. Did you find a new singer or did the band just fold? If you found one, I'll try to imagine him. What does the person who took my place look like? Does he resemble me or is he totally different? Is he at least a little thankful that I saved him a place until I left? Or doesn't he know about me at all since you don't talk about me, like we don't talk to new girlfriends about our old ones? Pero, you probably easily got in a few years of philosophy, maybe even graduated? It seems to me a whole eternity has passed since they took me away, so you surely had enough time to. I can just see you walking from the college to the Konzorcij bookstore. You let that goat's beard go that most of the college guys try to grow out, you carry your books in a leather police bag you begged from that uncle of yours, what's his name, and you undoubtedly have some kind of funny cap on your head, probably African, so people can see you're with them, that you're a brother to all, even the blacks (then why aren't you my brother anymore?). You walk slowly and smoke a cigarette, you're not in a hurry to get anywhere, you never have to run, let alone zigzag, in an irregular rhythm to mess up the sniper looking at you through a scope. You know, if you run regularly, sooner or later he'll get your rhythm and then, slowly breathing out to completely still his hands, he'll send a bullet into the back of your head or your back. You don't have to deal with banal questions like whether or not you'll cross that four-lane road alive. You think about totally different things. You think about the humanities department library and whether you'll again meet that cute one you noticed there yesterday, and whether you'll manage to build on that smile you gave her yesterday when as if by coincidence you reached for the same book. You think about the best ice breaker you'll disarm her with so as to continue the conversation in the nearest coffee shop where you'll go after each of you buys precisely the book you think will impress the other, and then she'll invite you from the coffee shop straight to her dorm room with a very clear hint that her roommate is in classes all afternoon and you'll be able to fuck her wildly, so wildly that you'll have to hold a hand over her mouth so they don't hear her out on the street. When she tells you to stay a while longer, you'll think something up, like you have a test to study for; you'll make your way back downtown, maybe to the Rio (if it's still open, or to some other getaway students with beards like), where you'll order a tall beer and page through the book you bought that afternoon in some corner. You're not in a hurry to go home, where there's only your mum, who always wants to talk a little. That gets on your nerves, you think about moving out, renting a room or a small flat, but you don't have the balls or the money, so you'll stay in your childhood room even later, when you get a job, which she'll arrange for you through connections.

Goran, sorry, old buddy, but I just can't manage to think of you any differently than in that Diamond manager's outfit, although I'm sure you're already past selling laundry and dish detergents and you're on the trail towards bigger money, which you so much like to feel between your fingers. Doubtless you're driving some outrageous car always flawlessly polished on the outside and fragrant on the inside. You're at the fitness club an hour or so a day, because you're convinced you have to take care of your body at least as much as your car, which in your case is a lot. Sooner or later you'll go abroad for a year because you were always so fascinated by the idea, and maybe you'll even stay. As I'm writing this, I can't help but conclude we never had anything in common aside from the North Side, where we grew up, aside from the neighbourhood we ran in. We didn't read the same books, we didn't watch the same films, we didn't listen to the same music, and we didn't laugh at the same jokes, but I still thought of you as one of my closest friends. All in all, besides comics, even they count, you didn't really read a lot. How many times did I excitedly loan you books I just finished reading so we could share the excitement, but you always gave up before the end. You couldn't even finish *Last Stop in Brooklyn* or a Beatles' biography, much less something like Kafka. The only book I know you read during all those years was Charles Bukowski's *Women*. For obvious reasons. But don't worry about it. Here, in this steaming cauldron of a country, I've concluded that people vastly overvalue reading and its supposedly positive effects. There are no guarantees. You wouldn't believe me if I started telling you how handy a student of comparative literature is with a knife and how enthusiastically a professor of philosophy fires a recoilless howitzer that works. He feels no empathy for the people he's firing at, only the pain of a nation that was wronged for centuries, so he keeps on loading one shell after another without rest. Fuck that. Fuck the nation that reduces you to an artilleryman on a hill.

Even rock 'n roll failed us. There's nothing left of what it promised. There's no fourth estate here, the rock 'n roll nation that would stand aside and not play like this war doesn't exist. No. All of us are in t-shirts of our favourite bands, acted just like everybody else and we all let ourselves be chosen by one of the three tribal teams. We're no better and no different from the rest, no matter that we looked down on what was coming until the last minute and pretended it had nothing to do with us and it wouldn't turn into this pile of shit just because we'd live our neutral rock 'n roll life to the end and make ugly faces at the hicks with the flags. When the draft bell rang, we joined one of the teams as if hypnotized. It's not surprising that Milan died. He had to die, from sorrow when he started recognizing faces he had seen beneath concert stages, in TV news clips from battlefields dressed in uniforms of the armies that are bumping around in these hills. You can only die of sorrow, what else is left when you see the idiotically smiling face of a man in camouflage in front of a levelled youth concert hall where you once played several sold-out concerts, and not long ago he was in the crowd below the stage singing the refrains of your songs along with you. Who was I singing to, who was I singing to all those years? Fuck rock 'n roll if you don't get the lyrics.

You remember our last time at the seaside? The last evening before we went home, totally despairing of the whole scene? When we had a smoke with that hippy type and his really bad ass wife, with whom

Goran, fucking ladies' man, disappeared at one point for a time and then returned with that cretin just-got-laid grin of his, while she had lost her bra and had grass in her hair? Pero, you and the hippy didn't notice a thing, you were so into each other that I was afraid you'd disappear from the table, too, and I'd be left all alone. The whole night, the guy rolled one joint after another, talking about the novel *Siddhartha* the entire time. About how it had opened his eyes, and he had become a new person and was going to devote his life to a spiritual journey on which he would go from city to city, village to village, person to person in search of spiritual brothers and sisters, liberated from the curse of material goods. You listened to him, Pero, more and more stoned, and even encouraged him because, yeah, that's the only sensible life, man! And he had to read the Slovene variant, Evald Flisar's *The Sorcerer's Apprentice*, because it's for sure at least as good as Hesse although you never really read it yourself, but your mum did, and everything you knew about it was from her recommending and loaning the book to neighbours, girlfriends, and relatives.

Why do I bring up the hippy?

Because I saw him, the damn bullshitting dick, a few weeks ago when he was liberating electronics, wires and cables from an empty house. He raised my hackles and I went up and asked him, 'Heh, pal, long time no see, is this part of the trip you lectured us on for a whole fucking evening?' 'What evening?' 'The evening one of my friends fucked your wife when you were going at it with my other friend.' (Sorry, Pero!) He looked at me dumbly, he probably thought I'd taken some shrapnel in the head and I could see he didn't have a clue what I was talking about, but I felt good.

The more I write, the angrier I get. Maybe it's time to wrap up. I don't know whether I'll ever send this letter, but the writing has reconnected me with you after these several years. It's a strange feeling. Bittersweet. There's probably some point in space and time where we'll meet again, a point where everything will again fall into place, a point of total balance. It has to exist, otherwise the whole thing would make no sense. I, for example, imagine it as a shelter, a nuclear, hermetically sealed one that guarantees complete isolation from the rest of the world. Windowless, with no phone, radio, or television. Antarctica. How will you know you found it? Doubtless I'll get there first and be waiting for you. Take your time, you don't have to hurry, beyond our meeting I don't have any plans for the future. I can wait a very long time. Maybe I'll write some song while I'm waiting. I haven't done that for a long time. Since I put on this camouflage crap, actually. They clearly don't go together, a uniform and poetry.. I don't yet have a title for the song, but for sure it will be a ballad. Essentially about Mary and me. About a couple who didn't have the slightest chance. I blamed myself for a long time, and that damn newsstand, and thought about how the road might have led past her to some other reality that I missed by mistake. I no longer think so. Now I know that all my roads led precisely here, otherwise why would someone stage this absurd script if not for me to act in it. This is my role. This is my lot. They won't be cast again, so I have nothing left but to play it out. Until the lights go down and it's check out time.

All the best,

*Denis.*

*Somewhere in the Balkans, 3 December 1994.*

# THE AUTHOR

**DINO BAUK** is a practising lawyer and a columnist for various leading Slovenian newspapers, including the prominent weekly, *Mladina*. He wrote a number of short stories before bursting onto the literary scene with his debut novel *The End. And Again* (*Konec. Znova*, 2015). The novel received the prestigious Best Debut Award of the Slovenian Book Fair and was longlisted for the Kresnik Award for best novel of the year, as well as being translated into Croatian, Serbian and German editions.

# THE TRANSLATOR

**TIMOTHY POGAČAR** is a faculty member in the Department of World Languages and Cultures at Bowling Green State University, USA, where he teaches Russian language, translation, and courses on post-socialist European societies. He edits (1995–) the journal *Slovene Studies*. Among his book- length (Slovene-English) translations are six novels by Evald Flisar and scholarly books by Marko Juvan (*Intertextuality: History and Poetics*, 2009) and Luka Vidmar (*A Slavic Republic of Letters: The Correspondence between Bartholomäus Kopitar and Sigismund Zois*, 2015).

www.ingramcontent.com/pod-product-compliance
Lightning Source LLC
Chambersburg PA
CBHW030130260626
47156CB00008B/2870